THE UNINTENTIONAL ADVENTURES
OF THE
BLAND SISTERS

← The Jolly Regina →

by Kara LaReau

Illustrated by Jen Hill

AMULET BOOKS
NEW YORK

Cataloging-in-Publication Data has been applied for and may be obtained from the Library of Congress.

ISBN: 978-1-4197-2605-7

Text copyright © 2017 Kara LaReau
Jacket and interior illustrations copyright © 2017 Jen Hill
Book design by Pamela Notarantonio

Printed and bound in U.S.A.
10 9 8 7 6 5 4 3 2 1

Amulet Books are available at special discounts when purchased in quantity for premiums and promotions as well as fundraising or educational use. Special editions can also be created to specification. For details, contact specialsales@abramsbooks.com or the address below.

ABRAMS The Art of Books
195 Broadway, New York, NY 10007
abramsbooks.com

For CRB, my very own unintentional adventure
—K.L.

THE UNINTENTIONAL CAST OF CHARACTERS

JAUNDICE   KALE

DELILAH

LEFTY

SMOKEY

PRINCESS

FATIMA

CAPTAIN ANN TENNILLE

MILLIE MUDD

PEG

tepid |'tepid| *adjective*
(esp. of a liquid) only
slightly warm

Chapter One

I f you ever find yourself on the road to Dullsville, you might
encounter an unassuming house. In it reside the Bland
Sisters, Jaundice and Kale.

You might tell the Bland Sisters apart in several ways.

First, Jaundice prefers to dress in gray, while Kale favors
brown.

Second, Kale wears her hair parted on the side, while
Jaundice parts hers in the middle.

Third, Jaundice is left-handed while Kale is right-handed.

Fourth, Kale is seldom seen without her backpack, in
which she currently carries *Dr. Nathaniel Snoote's Illustrated*

Children's Dictionary, a rather large leather-bound tome with a cracked spine reinforced with many layers of tape, a gold-stamped cover featuring the beatific silhouette of Dr. Snoote himself, and tabs along the side for each letter of the alphabet. The dictionary is the Bland Sisters' favorite reading material, and their main source of education. Carrying Dr. Snoote in her backpack is Kale's main source of physical *and* mental exercise.

Fifth, Jaundice is known to wear a smock featuring an inordinate number of pockets. Being the more skilled seamstress of the two sisters (a skill learned from one of Dr. Snoote's Educational Sidebars, called *Know Your Stitches*), Jaundice sewed this garment herself out of an old curtain and the upholstery of a long-since-discarded couch. Usually the pockets contain such treasures as a sock-darning needle and thread, several milk bottle caps, a long shoelace with various knots tied in it, and half of yesterday's sandwich wrapped in a napkin. Jaundice tends to forget to empty her pockets before her smock goes into the wash, much to the chagrin of Kale, who does the laundry.

Other than these few distinctions, the Bland Sisters are just about the same.

Jaundice and Kale pride themselves on their exacting routine. After breakfast (plain oatmeal with skim milk, a cup of weak, tepid tea on the side) they tend to their business of darning other people's socks, which takes the better part of the day. Each allows herself one ten-minute break, during which she eats a cheese sandwich on day-old bread and drinks a glass of flat soda while gazing out the window, watching the grass grow.

The Bland Sisters look forward most to the evenings, when they entertain themselves by reading the dictionary to each other, then staring at the wallpaper until they fall asleep.

It should be mentioned that Jaundice and Kale have parents. Several years ago, they left quite suddenly to run an errand of an unspecified nature. The Bland Sisters don't tend to dwell on it too much, as they are sure their parents will return any day now.

trying |ˈtrī-ng| *adjective*
annoying or difficult

———————— **Chapter Two** ————————

Jaundice?" said Kale one afternoon.

"Yes, Kale," said Jaundice.

"I have a Feeling," said Kale.

Jaundice sighed. Kale was always having Feelings. It was very trying.

"I have a Feeling," said Kale, "that something is going to happen."

"Of course, something is going to happen," said Jaundice, taking a fresh sock-darning needle from one of her pockets. "Something is always going to happen. Your telling me that something is going to happen is a happening, in and of itself."

Kale sighed. Jaundice was always dismissing her. It was very trying.

"Well, we're just about to finish the P section of the dictionary," offered Jaundice. "I know how you love the P section. Also, we have new cheese for our sandwiches."

"No," said Kale. "This is different. Something different is going to happen."

"Did I mention the cheese is white, instead of yellow?" said Jaundice.

Kale picked up another sock. It was no use explaining.

Suddenly, there was a knock at the door. The Bland Sisters looked at each other. No one came to the door. Ever. Not even to deliver the cheese—the grocer left that in a basket by the mailbox, along with other sundries, like toothbrushes and laundry powder and sock-darning thread.

"What shall we do?" asked Kale.

"I'm not sure," said Jaundice. "Let me think."

"Let's pretend we're sleeping," said Kale. "Maybe they'll go away."

This was Kale's solution for any moment of relative peril. She closed her eyes, tilted her head to one side, and began fake-snoring. Jaundice followed suit.

The knocking only grew louder.

"It's not working," whispered Jaundice.

"Shh," said Kale.

Knock-knock. Knock-knock. Knock-knock-knock.

"It's still not working," whispered Jaundice.

"Zzzzzzzzzz," said Kale.

"I have a radical idea," said Jaundice. She stood up. She walked to the door.

"You can't be serious," said Kale.

But she was. Jaundice was always serious.

"Who is it?" she asked.

Finally, the knocking stopped.

"It's a surprise!" a cheerful voice said.

predicament |pri'dikəmənt| *noun*
an unpleasant, embarrassing, or
difficult situation

Chapter Three

The Bland Sisters looked at each other.

"I didn't order anything surprising," said Jaundice. "Did you?"

Kale shook her head.

"What is it?" she asked The Voice Behind the Door.

"I can't tell you," The Voice said sweetly. "That's what makes it a *surprise.*"

"I have a Feeling," said Kale.

Jaundice sighed. Here we go *again*, she thought.

"I have a Feeling we should open the door," said Kale.

"We can't," said Jaundice. "You know the rule."

"Which one?" Kale asked.

In the absence of parental supervision, the Bland Sisters had established many rules. One was: Don't Use More than One Slice of Cheese on Your Sandwich. Another was: Don't Part Your Hair on the Side If You Usually Part It in the Middle, and Vice Versa. A third was: When in a Moment of Relative Peril, Pretend You're Sleeping.

But Jaundice had a different rule in mind.

"Never Open the Door to Strangers," she said.

"Right," said Kale. "I'd forgotten about that one."

She addressed the door again.

"We don't open the door to strangers," she informed The Voice.

For a few moments, the Bland Sisters heard nothing. Then The Voice cleared its throat.

"I guess you won't be getting your surprise, then," it said. "I need you to sign for it."

"Well," said Kale. "This is a predicament."

"Not really," said Jaundice, after giving the situation some thought. "We *could* bend our rule, just this once. After all, there's only one of them and two of us. If it means us any harm, we'll outnumber it."

Kale wasn't sure what Jaundice meant, as she wasn't

very good at numbers. *Math Is Fun*, Dr. Snoote's sidebar on mathematics, was very long and involved, and it always gave her a headache. But Kale nodded in agreement anyway.

Jaundice, being good at numbers (and not being as prone to mathematically induced headaches), counted to three. Then she opened the door.

On the other side, most definitely, was a surprise.

insignia |inˈsignēə| *noun*
a badge, mark, or
emblem of official rank
or membership

Chapter Four

On the doorstep of the Bland Sisters' house was a woman with only one hand. The Bland Sisters surmised this fact because she was wearing a sharp metal hook where her left hand should be. The woman had a black bandanna tied on her head and large hoop earrings in her ears. Her shirt was white and ruffly and cinched with a wide leather belt, and she wore black silk pants tucked into tall black boots. On her belt was an insignia of a skull and crossbones.

"Well," said Jaundice. "That's certainly a look."

"I've seen that insignia before," Kale said. "Somewhere."

"Are ye the Bland Sisters?" the woman asked.

"We are," said Jaundice. "Where is our surprise?"

The woman brought something out from behind her back.

"Is that burlap?" Kale exclaimed, clapping her hands. "Burlap is my all-time favorite fabric."

"It's a sack," said Jaundice. "A burlap sack."

"Ye must be the smart one," the woman said. She smiled, revealing several gold teeth.

Jaundice blushed. She *was* the smart one. In her opinion, at least.

"So where is the surprise?" Kale asked.

"Inside," the woman said, opening the sack just a bit.

The Bland Sisters peered in.

"I don't see anything," said Kale.

"Me, neither," said Jaundice.

"Ye have to look closer," the woman said, shaking the sack. "It's at the bottom."

The Bland Sisters leaned in.

"Closer," the woman said.

They leaned in farther.

"I think I see something," Jaundice said.

"Me, too," said Kale. "More burlap!"

"Gotcha," said the woman. She drew up the sack and tied it shut, then threw it over her shoulder with remarkable ease.

The Bland Sisters were trapped.

"I just remembered something," said Jaundice, her voice muffled in the folds of burlap. "I don't like surprises."

"Me, neither," said Kale. "Especially this kind."

burlap |ˈbərlap| *noun*
coarse fabric woven
from hemp or jute

Chapter Five

For a long while, the Bland Sisters were kept in the dark about what the woman was up to, because they *were* in the dark. Literally.

"Burlap is not as nice as it looks," Kale whispered as they bounced along. "It's actually quite chafing."

"Tell me about it," Jaundice said.

"I hope they have some salve on hand, wherever we're going," said Kale.

"Where *do* you think we're going?" Jaundice asked.

"I couldn't guess," said Kale.

She really couldn't. For as long as they could remember,

neither of the Bland Sisters had ever been anywhere, other than to the mailbox to fetch their weekly basket of sundries.

"Pipe down," the woman said. Her voice was not nearly as sweet as it had been before. "We're almost there."

It was at this point that the Bland Sisters began to notice a Terrible Smell.

"Is that you?" Kale asked.

"Certainly not," said Jaundice.

"Ah!" the woman said, inhaling deeply. "Like perfume, it is."

"It must have been her," said Jaundice.

"Heavens," said Kale. "She must have a *serious* digestive problem."

It was at this point that the Bland Sisters began to notice an Unusual Noise.

"Do you hear that?" Jaundice asked.

"I do," said Kale. "It sounds like someone splashing around in the bathtub."

"A very, very big bathtub," Jaundice said.

"Here we are!" the woman announced.

And with that, she let the sack drop to the floor. The Bland Sisters landed with a thud.

"Oof," said Jaundice.

"Ouch," said Kale.

Within seconds, the sack was opened. At first, the Bland Sisters thought the sun was playing tricks on their eyes. The sun always seemed so harsh and bright and had a tendency to illuminate things so very much; up till now, Jaundice and Kale preferred to avoid its direct glare whenever possible. They both blinked for a good long while to make sure they were seeing correctly. Because what they were seeing was that they were sitting on the deck of a ship. And what they were smelling was the distinct, briny aroma of the ocean.

The Bland Sisters had never been to the ocean before, so the sensory experience was considerably overwhelming.

"It's so . . . so . . . *blue*," said Kale.

"And *big*," said Jaundice. "Like the sky, only lower and wavier."

Above the Bland Sisters loomed a tall woman with long red hair, dressed all in red and black, from her tricorn hat to her high, laced-up boots. On one eye, she wore a black velvet patch bejeweled with a skull and crossbones.

"Welcome to *The Jolly Regina*, lassies!" the woman said. "You're Deadeye Delilah's swabs now!" She put her hands on her hips and laughed heartily. The skull and crossbones on her eye patch sparkled in the sun. "Let's weigh anchor, mateys!"

"Now I remember where I saw that insignia before," Kale said, reaching for Dr. Snoote and flipping through the pages.

"Oh?" said Jaundice.

"It was here, in the P section," Kale said. "Next to the definition of *pirate*."

"Ah," said Jaundice, watching the ship pull away from the dock. "Then I can think of another appropriate P word."

peril |ˈperəl| *noun*
extreme and
immediate danger

Chapter Six

That was the P word Jaundice uttered: *Peril.* On the Peril Continuum, the Bland Sisters had gone from encountering Relative Peril to experiencing Serious, Life-Threatening Peril.

So what did the sisters do? You guessed it.

They slumped to the floor and began fake-snoring.

As ever, this tactic proved futile.

"Get up, ye lazyboneses!" shouted Deadeye Delilah. She grabbed Jaundice's and Kale's heads and rapped them together, which elicited a sound not unlike the knocking together of coconuts.

After seeing stars for a few seconds, the sisters helped each other up. That's when they noticed the rest of the crew looking at them.

"Women can be pirates?" Kale asked, thumbing through her dictionary. "Dr. Snoote doesn't say anything about that in the definition of *pirate*.

Or in the definition of *women*." In fact, all the pirates in front of them were women.

"Then ye'd best not trust yer dictionary, missy," Delilah said.

"The men don't want anyone to know about us," said the woman with a hook for a left hand. "They don't like to admit having their loot plundered by a bunch of saucy wenches."

The rest of the crew laughed. The hook-handed woman came closer.

"M'name's Lefty," she growled. She extended her hook to Jaundice and Kale, then pulled it away with a smirk and offered her good hand.

"Jaundice Bland," said Jaundice. "And this is my sister, Kale."

"Right good pirate names," said a woman with a wooden leg.

"And your name is?" asked Kale.

"Peg."

"Who's got Scurvy? Who's got Scurvy?" Deadeye Delilah bellowed, until a tiny monkey wearing a red vest was brought to her. "There he is, me little bucko."

Scurvy perched on Delilah's shoulder, allowing her to kiss him right on the lips. In return, he handed her a shiny gray button, which Jaundice immediately recognized.

"Hey," she said, looking down at the jagged hole in her smock where the button used to be. "That's mine."

"Everything of yers is Deadeye Delilah's now," Deadeye Delilah said. "Yer both mine now, see? That's the deal."

"I don't remember making any deal," Jaundice said. "Do you, Kale?"

"No," said Kale. "All I remember is the promise of a surprise. And then, a lot of burlap."

Kale consulted her dictionary again. Surely some answers could be found in Dr. Snoote's definition of *deal*, or *surprise*, or *pirate*. Or *burlap*.

"Oh, the deal wasn't with ye, missies," said Deadeye Delilah. "It was with yer parents."

"Our *parents?!*" Jaundice exclaimed. Kale's eyes widened. Neither she nor her sister had ever spoken at such a volume.

Scurvy bobbed his head up and down and began screeching.

spyglass |ˈspīˌglas| *noun*
a small telescope

←——————— **Chapter Seven** ———————→

As you might imagine, there weren't any answers to the Bland Sisters' questions in the dictionary or otherwise.

"Our parents are off running an errand, aren't they?" Jaundice asked Kale.

"*Are* they?" Kale asked. "I can't seem to recall. It was so long ago."

Jaundice and Kale took a moment to think. It had been a while since they'd thought about their parents; over the years, the Bland Sisters had found so many other ways to occupy their time.

"They were there with us at home, at one point," Jaundice said. "And then they weren't. That's all I know."

"All I know is that you two had better get to work," growled Lefty. "Grab a brush and a bucket, and get scrubbin'."

Lefty, as it turned out, was Deadeye Delilah's first mate, which meant she ran the crew while Delilah steered the ship and looked out at the horizon with a spyglass. It was a good career choice for Lefty, as it was hard to argue with a person with a hook for a hand.

Of course, Jaundice and Kale had never done more than sock darning and chores at home, where everything was safe and familiar and well shaded, so scrubbing the decks of a pirate ship on their hands and knees in the blazing sun did not come easily to them. In fact, they found it quite draining, even after only four or five hours.

"My skin is hot and sweaty," whined Kale.

"My back is sore," moaned Jaundice.

"My ears hurt," yelled Lefty. "Quit yer yappin' or I'll give you the cat."

"There's a cat here, *and* a monkey?" Jaundice said.

"Ooh, I think I might like cats," Kale said wistfully. "Why didn't we ever have one?"

"It's not that kind of cat," whispered Peg. "She means a *cat-o'-nine-tails*. Ye don't want to be messin' with that, so work faster."

The Bland Sisters noticed a whip with nine lashes hanging from Lefty's belt on the left side. It looked as if it would hurt. A lot.

"On second thought, I don't like cats," Kale said with a shudder. "Not at all."

"Oh, there's far worse than the cat, ye can be sure," Peg explained. "There's the Jack Ketch, the keelhaul, and there's always a good marooning. Though I'm sure you two know about marooning better than ole Peg."

The Bland Sisters barely understood a word of what Peg said, but they smiled and nodded anyway, just to be polite. In truth, all they knew about pirates was what they read in the dictionary. Kale reviewed the definition, just to be sure.

"What about walking the plank?" Kale offered. That was the only thing Dr. Snoote said about pirate justice: Pirates forced you to walk along a plank, fall into the water, and surely drown. The supplementary illustration for this was particularly dramatic.

"No truth to it," Peg said, spitting over the side. "I never seen a plank-walkin' in all me years."

"This dictionary needs a bit of updating," Kale said.

"Clearly," said Jaundice.

Just then, the Bland Sisters heard a horrible *SNAP!* They jumped back, as did Peg, just in time to escape the whip of the cat-o'-nine-tails. Lefty stood over them, gesturing with her hook.

"No time fer chitchat, bilge rats!" she growled, strutting away.

"That was close," Kale whispered.

"Blimey," Peg said. "I nearly soiled me poop deck."

booty |ˈbo͞otē| *noun*
a valuable prize, usually
taken by force

Chapter Eight

"SAIL HO! SAIL HO!" cried a voice from above.

The Bland Sisters looked up. A girl not much older than they were was sitting in the crow's nest, waving her arms. Everyone on deck dropped what they were doing and stared out at the horizon.

"What's going on?" asked Jaundice.

"That's Millie Mudd up there," said Peg. "She's our lookout. Must be a ship approaching."

Deadeye Delilah gazed through her spyglass and chuckled. She handed it to Lefty, who took a look for herself and started chuckling, too.

"Looks like we got ourselves an easy target, me hearties," Delilah announced to the crew. "It's *The Testostero*."

"Everyone get into character. Ye know the drill," advised Lefty. At this, the crew members began hiding their weapons, fluffing up their hair, and washing the dirt off their faces. Someone passed around a vial of perfume, which everyone made sure to apply. Except for the Bland Sisters, of course.

"Don't ye want some par-foom?" Peg asked.

"No, thank you," Kale said, passing the bottle along. "We don't use cosmetics."

"Too bad," Peg said, dabbing a generous amount behind her ears. "You two could use some sprucin' up."

Eventually, *The Testostero* came into view. It was a much smaller ship than the *Regina*, but it had very large bloodred sails.

"They're all men," Kale remarked, sizing up the crew.

"They seem much dirtier than the illustrations of pirates in our dictionary," noted Jaundice.

The *Testostero*'s captain came forward and called out to the *Regina*.

"Ahoy!" he said cheerfully, lifting his hat. When he smiled, he revealed a mouth full of gold teeth. "Me name's Captain Jerry."

"Well, *helloooo*, Jerry," Delilah purred. "Me name's Delilah."

"And me name's Barry," said Captain Jerry's bespectacled first mate. "Ye know, the high seas is no place for lovely lassies like yerselves."

"Ohhh, yer so right, ye are," said Lefty, in a high-pitched voice. "We'd *much* rather be cookin' or bakin' or sewin' than floatin' around on this ratty, horrible ship. Right, ladies?"

The rest of the crew of the *Regina* nodded in agreement. They batted their eyelashes, wrung their hands, tossed their hair, and giggled.

"Why is everyone acting so funny?" Jaundice asked.

"Shh," said Peg. "Just play along."

"Certainly, we'll be glad to escort ye to the nearest safe harbor," said Jerry. "Fer a modest fee."

"And we'll be glad to take yer ratty, horrible ship off yer hands, so ye can get back to yer womanly pursuits," said Barry.

"Yer *too* kind," cooed Delilah.

No sooner had the words left her mouth than the pirates of *The Testostero* were climbing aboard the *Regina*.

"They don't look any nicer close-up," Kale whispered.

"Or cleaner," said Jaundice.

"This is gonna be easy," Captain Jerry said to his crew, rubbing his hands together. "Like takin' candy from a baby. From a ship *full* o' babies."

"Arrrgh! Hand over yer treasure, lassies!" Barry growled, brandishing a little dagger.

"How 'bout ye hand over *yers*?" said Delilah, as the crew of the *Regina* revealed their impressive array of weapons.

"Uh-oh," said Jerry.

In one quick movement, Lefty brought her cat-o'-nine-tails out from behind her back and cracked it.

SNAP!

Barry's dagger flew out of his hand and went overboard.

"Me blade!" he cried.

"Yer lucky ye didn't lose yer little fingers, too, crybaby," Lefty said.

"No one makes me shipmates cry," snarled Captain Jerry, pulling out his sword. "Especially a girl."

Delilah pulled out her sword, too. "Well," she said, "there's a first time fer everything."

"I'm getting a Feeling," Kale said to her sister.

"Is it a Feeling that we're about to be in Relative Peril?" Jaundice asked.

"Exactly," said Kale. "You know the drill."

Had the Bland Sisters not closed their eyes and slumped to the floor in pretend sleep, they would have been privy to an incredible showing of swordplay by Delilah and a stunning all-out brawl between the crews of the *Regina* and *The Testostero*. Unfortunately for the men, they were quickly overpowered.

"That'll teach ye to underestimate us wenches," said Lefty, spitting at *The Testostero*'s crew. "Now, we'll help ourselves to yer booty!"

"Hurrah!" cheered the crew of the *Regina*, as they all boarded the enemy ship and stripped it of all its gold, its food, its ale, its livestock, and its weapons. They even took its sails. Afterward, they forced *The Testostero*'s crew back onto its deck.

"Please don't kill us!" Captain Jerry pleaded, his mouth now slack and toothless.

"Oh, we feel sorry for ye boys, so we're not going to kill ye," announced Delilah. "What we are going to do is set ye adrift without yer sails. And we'd like yer captain to surrender his pants."

"What's that?" said Captain Jerry.

"Ye heard the lady," Lefty said, waving her cat-o'-nine-tails. "Give us yer pants, or we're gonna whoop yer bums again."

When the Bland Sisters finally opened their eyes, they saw *The Testostero*, now without its sails, and its captain, now shivering in his long johns, floating away. The crew of *The Jolly Regina* laughed and waved.

"Toodle-oo, boys!" Lefty shouted.

"Thanks for the memories!" added Delilah, blowing a kiss. Together, she and Lefty hoisted Captain Jerry's pants up the *Regina's* flagpole.

Jaundice looked up, squinting. "Yikes," she said.

"What?" asked Kale, following her sister's gaze. "Oh, my."

Flapping in the breeze at the top of the flagpole, along with Captain Jerry's pants, were many other pairs. The Bland Sisters tried to count them, but there were too many.

"What are ye gapin' at?" Lefty snarled, snapping her cat-o'-nine-tails. "Get back to work, scrubs!"

Jaundice and Kale scrambled to find their brushes and buckets and quickly resumed their hard labor, not wanting to raise the ire of their pirate hosts. After all, the crew of *The Jolly Regina* were not only pillagers and plunderers. They were also ruthless depantsers.

doubloons |dəˈblo͞ons| *plural noun*
historical Spanish gold coins

Chapter Nine

As the sun was setting, Lefty ordered the deckhands to stop their scrubbing.

"Finally," Jaundice said, removing half of yesterday's cheese sandwich from one of her smock pockets and taking a bite. "I could use a break."

"Me, too. And some of that sandwich," said Kale.

Jaundice tore the sandwich in half. But before she could hand Kale her portion, Scurvy leaped up and snatched both pieces.

"Hey!" shouted Jaundice. "That was mine!"

"And mine!" added Kale.

In response, Scurvy screeched, stuffed the sandwich in his mouth, and scampered away.

Jaundice sighed.

"Monkeys are the worst," she decided. Wearily, Kale nodded in agreement.

"Delilah wants to see the two of ye," Lefty growled, grabbing them both by their tired arms and pushing them toward the captain's quarters. Jaundice and Kale could barely stand, let alone protest.

When they arrived, Deadeye Delilah was relaxing in a hammock made of *The Testostero*'s red sails, drinking from a jug of rum. A table in front of her was covered with the spoils of the day's plundering: gold doubloons, pieces of eight, and Captain Jerry's gold teeth. Scurvy was lying next to Delilah, playing with one of her braids. When he saw Jaundice, he stuck out his tongue. Her button was already pinned to his vest like a medal.

"They're all yours, me hearty," Lefty said.

"Due south," Delilah ordered. "We'll reach Port Innastorm in three days. Then we can trade in some of this booty and treat ourselves to a good time."

Lefty gave the captain a wink, then went back upstairs.

Delilah shrugged. "Someone's got to steer the ship while I splice the main brace, so to speak." She took another swig.

At this point, the Bland Sisters began to notice another Terrible Smell: the smell of a rum-soaked pirate queen.

"Don't breathe through your nose," advised Jaundice.

"I'm way ahead of you," whispered Kale.

"So tell me," Deadeye Delilah said. "What do ye ladies know about treasure?"

Kale took out her dictionary and thumbed through to the T section.

"Um," she said. "It's 'a quantity of something valuable'?"

" . . . 'such as gems, or metals,'" said Jaundice, reading over her sister's shoulder. "'Or other precious items.'"

"Don't play games with me, missies," Delilah snarled. "Ye know what treasure I'm talkin' about. Cap'n Tennille's treasure."

"Captain Tennille?" Jaundice asked.

"Captain Ann Tennille," Deadeye Delilah said. "She was the greatest pirate on the seven seas. Before yers truly, anyway. I was her first mate when I was barely older than ye. And she had a ship full of treasure, ten times as much as this pittance from *The Testostero*. Why, Cap'n Ann had the biggest booty ye ever laid eyes on!"

The Bland Sisters tried to imagine this, with mixed results.

Delilah took another swig of rum. "And then, one day, she caught me stealin'. 'No one pinches Cap'n Ann's booty,'

she says. That's when she sent me floating off on a raft.
Didn't have the heart to feed me to the fish, bless her heart.
But she set me adrift, all the same. So I vowed to find her,
someday, somehow, and take all her treasure for meself. I'm
going to prove to her, once and fer all, who's the *real* pirate
queen."

Jaundice and Kale were riveted. This was much, much
more interesting than reading the dictionary. Delilah's
account was filled with interesting characters, an engaging
plot, and real conflict.

It was, in fact, a story. The first story they could ever remember hearing.

"And then what happened?" Kale asked.

"Aw, ye both know what happened," Delilah grumbled.

"We want to hear you tell it," said Jaundice, giving her sister a look.

"Well, I got me own ship and me own crew and started sailin' 'round the world, lookin' for Ann. That's when I came across yer parents. They said they knew all about Ann and her treasure and where she was hidin' out, and they wanted to share it with me if I let them use *The Jolly Regina* to find it."

"And then what?" the Bland Sisters said at the same time, surprising themselves.

"And then what?" Delilah took another drink of rum. "And then I double-crossed them, that's what. I had Lefty tie 'em up and then I told 'em to tell me where to find the treasure, or else."

"Did they tell you?" Jaundice asked.

"They told me it was on Gilly Guns Island, so that's where we went. And do you know what we found?"

"Treasure?" Kale guessed.

"No," said Delilah. "A whole lot of nothin'. So I told yer parents they had to face pirates' justice: either Jack Ketch, which is a good hangin'; the keelhaul, which is a draggin' and drownin'; or maroonin', which is abandonin' without food or water. Their choice."

Jaundice swallowed hard. "So which did they pick?" she asked. None of the options sounded very good, really.

"I'll tell ye the one they *didn't* pick," Delilah said. "They begged me, 'Oh, Captain Delilah, *please* don't maroon us here on the island! *Anything* but that!' So guess which one they got?"

"Marooning?" Kale offered.

"Right-o," Delilah said. "Ye must be the smart one."

Kale blushed. She *was* the smart one. In her own opinion, at least.

"They even told me I could have ye two as my scrubs, if I promised not to maroon 'em," Delilah added. "A lot of good it did them, *heh heh* . . . "

And us, the Bland Sisters thought at the same time.

diatribe |ˈdīəˌtrīb| *noun*
an angry speech

— Chapter Ten —

It became very clear to the Bland Sisters that Deadeye
Delilah had enjoyed her share of rum for the night.
This was a conclusion reached after Delilah trailed off
midsentence, dropped her empty jug, and immediately began
snoring, openmouthed.

In fact, Scurvy was inebriated by association; he'd kept his
face too close to Delilah's mouth and grew drunk from the
rum fumes alone. Jaundice leaned in and carefully, carefully
removed her button from his little vest.

"That'll teach you to steal from *me*, sea monkey," Jaundice
whispered. She pulled out her sock-darning needle and thread

from one of her smock pockets and sewed the button back on with impressive speed.

"Do you have anything in your other pockets?" Kale asked.

"Good question," said Jaundice.

Upon further investigation, it was determined that Jaundice was in possession of the following items:

A sock-darning needle and thread, as previously mentioned

A kitchen magnet

A stick, burned at one end, used by Jaundice to poke the logs in the fire at home

A crumpled napkin, in which the aforementioned cheese sandwich remnant (cruelly snatched by Scurvy) had been wrapped

One rubber band

One thumbtack

One paper clip

"Well," Kale said, wrinkling her nose. "I'm just glad none of these bits and bobs ended up in the laundry this time. The *last* thing we need is needles and thumbtacks and paper clips and a magnet rattling around in the washing machine. Not to mention that dirty stick. Remember the time you left a half-eaten cheese sandwich in your pocket? Don't get me started on that fiasco. You try scrubbing melted cheese out of a load of wool socks . . ."

As Kale continued with her diatribe, Jaundice shoved her hands in two of her empty smock pockets and shut her eyes. Everything was so complicated now, being away from home, kidnapped by pirates, and kept as servants. And worse, the Bland Sisters' parents were most likely not off running an errand. More likely, they were in danger.

"What do you remember about our parents?" Jaundice asked.

Kale stopped complaining about the laundry. For a little while, she stared out into the middle distance, as she always did when she was deep in thought.

"Hmm," Kale said. "I seem to recall crying whenever our mother tried to coax us into venturing outside. The sun always felt so harsh and the flowers seemed too fragrant, and the laughter of other children hurt my ears."

"I remember our father attempting to serve something other than oatmeal for breakfast one morning," Jaundice said.

Both sisters shuddered.

"Well, I think they had good intentions," Kale noted.

"I think we need to have a plan," Jaundice said.

"A what?" asked Kale.

"A plan, for *rescuing them*," Jaundice said. Sometimes, Kale was a little slow on the uptake. "Why do you think our parents told Delilah where to find us?"

"Because they were willing to sacrifice us to save themselves?" Kale offered.

"No." Jaundice sighed. "Because they wanted to find a way to get us on *The Jolly Regina*, so we could find Gilly Guns Island and rescue them."

"I still don't understand," Kale said. "I thought our parents were running an errand."

"Somehow that errand led them here," Jaundice said. "And now they're missing."

"Marooned," Kale added.

"Right-o," Jaundice said. "Now you're getting the hang of it."

"But what can we do?" Kale said.

"I'm not completely sure," Jaundice said. "I've never devised a plan before."

ROWWWWWWWR.

"What was that?" Jaundice said.

"Sorry," Kale said, clutching her stomach. "Hunger pangs."

"Maybe we should find some food," Jaundice suggested. "If we eat, it might allow us to think more clearly."

"There isn't any food in here," Kale said, looking around Delilah's chamber. "Lots of jugs of rum, but no food."

"If only I had stowed something else in my smock that was edible, let alone useful," Jaundice said, scooping up a cork from an empty rum jug and slipping it into one of her pockets. She was always pocketing things, here and there, just as she'd

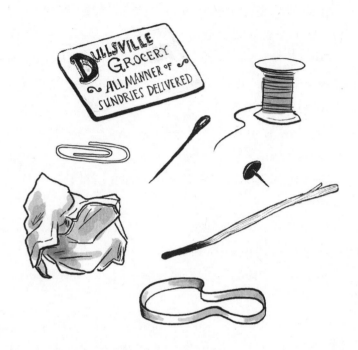

absentmindedly pocketed the kitchen magnet that morning after she'd used it to pick up some sock-darning needles she'd dropped. Jaundice was odd in that way, among many others.

"I miss our sundries basket," Kale said wistfully.

"Me, too," said Jaundice. "We never even got a chance to try the new cheese. It looked very promising."

"Even if there isn't any food here, I'd rather not leave this room," Kale said.

"Me, neither," said Jaundice. "It's comforting to stay in one place, surrounded by walls and a ceiling and a floor."

"Almost . . . like home," Kale said.

ROWWWWWWWWR.

"Oh, no. Not you, too," Jaundice said, looking down at her stomach. "I guess there's only one thing to do."

"Sleep?" offered Kale.

"No," said Jaundice. "Go out and look for food."

"Are you sure?" Kale asked.

"No," said Jaundice. "But my stomach is."

Slowly, quietly, the Bland Sisters tiptoed down the corridor and looked around until they found a door marked GALLEY.

"It's locked," Kale said, jiggling the knob. "We'll need to find the key."

"Fat chance of that," said Jaundice.

"You don't have a skeleton key in one of those pockets, do you?" asked Kale. "That would be terribly helpful."

"It would," said Jaundice, rooting around, then pulling out the paper clip. "But I might have something just as good."

As she had never attempted to pick a lock before, let alone with a paper clip, it took Jaundice an extended period of time to get the door open. But as they say, better late than never.

Inside the galley, the Bland Sisters found a long wooden table, stacks of pots and pans, and a row of barrels and sacks.

In one corner, a cauldron sat on a hearth. Jaundice reached out and touched the side of it cautiously.

"Whatever it is, it's still warm," she said. She lifted the lid.

The contents of the cauldron looked almost uniformly brown. Chunks of potatoes and unidentifiable meat floated in a greasy, beefy broth. Kale wrinkled her nose.

"That looks questionable," she said, though brown *was* her favorite color.

"What is it?" Jaundice asked.

"A stew . . . I think," said Kale, thumbing through Dr. Snoote to be sure. Neither sister had ever eaten anything more than oatmeal and cheese sandwiches, so they could only guess.

"I found these," said Jaundice, holding out two large crackers. "They seem a bit harder than our bread at home, but I think they'll do."

The Bland Sisters found two wooden bowls and scooped themselves some stew from the cauldron. They each sat on one of the barrels and ate, using the crackers to sop up the last bits. Kale would remember it as the most satisfying meal she'd ever had, mostly because she was so utterly famished.

"I'm not sure I like meat," announced Jaundice afterward. "It's tough and gristly, isn't it?"

"Just be glad we don't know what animal it came from," said Kale, patting her belly.

"True," said Jaundice. "Very true."

"Funny, you don't see very many rats on these pirate ships, do you?" Kale said. "It must be because of how clean they keep the decks. I would have thought there'd be rats everywhere."

"That's something to stew on, isn't it?" said Jaundice, letting out a little burp.

chantey |ˈshantē| *noun*
a song usually sung
by sailors

← —— Chapter Eleven —— →

After their questionable meal, the Bland Sisters tried to make their way back to Delilah's quarters. Unfortunately, their sense of direction was less than keen, and before long, Jaundice and Kale were lost.

"We're lost," said Jaundice, leaning against a ladder. "All the doors here look the same."

"I guess this is what they call a dead end," Kale said.

"If there were only some means of getting around that didn't involve a door," said Jaundice.

Kale rested her head on one of the ladder's rungs. "Like a window," she said.

"Or stairs," said Jaundice. "Or something stair-like."

The Bland Sisters took a moment to flirt with despair.

"It's too bad this ladder's no good," Kale said, sighing.

"What's wrong with it?" Jaundice asked, pressing against it to test its sturdiness.

"We have no idea where it goes," said Kale.

Jaundice rolled her eyes. "Of *course* we know where it goes," she said.

"We do? Where?" asked Kale.

"Obviously," said her sister, "it goes *up*."

Jaundice climbed up first and poked her head out.

"All clear," she said.

Not surprisingly, Jaundice was right. The ladder did go up. In fact, it led the Bland Sisters above deck. It was nighttime now, and the sky was filled with stars. Jaundice and Kale took a moment to take in the glittering array.

"The night sky looks different here than from our window at home," Kale said, tilting her head back.

"We don't get much of a view from our window at home," Jaundice said.

"It reminds me of our bedroom wallpaper," Kale said. "But sparklier."

Jaundice looked around the deck. "It's strange that no one is up here," she said. "Where is everyone? And where is that music coming from?"

It was true; there was loud music and singing and clapping coming from the other end of the ship, below deck. The sisters crept to the other end, lifted the overhead door, and peeked down. There, they saw what looked to be the entire crew assembled in a circle. In the center was Peg, playing a hornpipe, and a large woman in a stained apron, doing what appeared to be a jig.

"I bet that's the cook," Kale said.

The Jigging Woman Who Might Be the Cook was also singing a song—the Bland Sisters recognized it as a chantey, as defined by Dr. Snoote.

Ohhh we are some saucy beau-tees,
we rules the seven seas,
we steals the menfolk's booty
an' brings 'em to their knees.

Ohhh you'd best be wary, misters,
the seas are cold and deep,
so keep a lookout for me sisters
and hold yer booty whiles ye sleep!

Saucy beau-tees, yo-ho-ho!
Menfolks' booty, yo-ho-ho!

Wary, misters, yo-ho-ho!
Look out for me sisters—yo-HO!

"She's quite good," Kale said, though she wasn't a qualified judge. The Bland Sisters hadn't heard much by way of music while they were growing up; they did have a record player, but all they had ever played was a boxed set of public speaking records called *The Elegance of Eloquence with Mavis Diphthong*. And their radio had terrible reception. Kale got very good at discerning the subtle crackles and pops of static.

Jaundice, on the other hand, was not impressed. In her opinion, the might-be cook sounded like she had one of those hard crackers in her throat, and Peg was a bit slow with the beat, given that she was keeping time with her wooden leg.

"Encore, encore!" shouted Lefty, and the song started up again.

Great, thought Jaundice. Then she looked at Lefty and had a realization.

"Who's steering the ship?" she asked.

The sisters crept over to the ship's wheel. It was held fast with a rope.

"What's this?" Kale asked, producing a long tube of leather, tied loosely with a string. She untied it and unrolled the tube, revealing a very large, detailed map.

"Look," Jaundice said, placing her finger on a patch of land. "Here's Dullsville."

Kale traced her finger south, all the way down to the bottom of the page.

"And here's where Delilah said we were going," she said. "Due south, to Port Innastorm."

"But here's where we *want* to go," Jaundice said. "South*west*."

She pointed to a tiny speck in the middle of the ocean. Over the speck, someone had penciled in the letters GGI.

"Gilly Guns Island," Kale whispered.

It took the Bland Sisters some effort to absorb all of this information. It helped to focus on the starry sky above. Jaundice found that if she squinted, it really did look like their wallpaper at home.

"Are you having any thoughts?" Kale asked after a few minutes.

"I'm not sure," said Jaundice. "But I do have a plan."

"Do tell," said Kale, clapping her hands.

"Well, if we steer the ship to sail *west* each night, after everyone else goes to sleep, then steer it to sail *south* each morning, before everyone else wakes up, we'll secretly be headed *southwest*," Jaundice explained. "We'll be there in no time."

"But how do we know which way is south and which way is west?" asked Kale.

"Oh. Right," said Jaundice. "How do the pirates know?"

Kale flipped to the N section of the dictionary and looked up *navigation*.

"According to Dr. Snoote, we need to find the North Star. Wherever it is will be north," Kale explained. "We can figure out south and west from there. And east, if we have to."

The Bland Sisters looked up at the sky again. The wallpaper of constellations blinked down at them, beautiful and mysterious.

"All these stars look the same. What a stupid plan. Stupid, stupid, stupid," said Jaundice, kicking a barrel filled with rainwater.

"It isn't stupid. It's just not fully developed," said Kale, looking at the stars again for inspiration.

"Why did I have to fill my pockets with sock-darning needles and kitchen magnets?" said Jaundice. "Why couldn't I have brought something *useful*, like a compass?"

Kale's eyes grew wide.

"Oh," she said. "Wait."

She flipped to the C section of the dictionary, and thumbed over to the entry for *compass*. To the left was one of Dr. Snoote's many Educational Sidebars, called

Make Your Own Compass

❧ YOU'LL NEED ❧

 + a needle

+ a bar magnet

 + a cork

+ a cup of water

1. Rub the North end of the magnet against the point of the needle 20 times.
2. Rub the South end of the magnet against the eye of the needle 20 times.
3. Stick the needle all the way through the cork.
4. Float the cork in the cup of water. The needle will point North.

(in this case, a sock-darning needle)

(in this case, a kitchen magnet)

(in this case, a cork from a pirate queen's empty rum jug)

(in this case, a barrel filled with rainwater)

Once the compass showed Jaundice and Kale which direction was south, they determined which way was west. Jaundice steered the ship in that direction.

"Voilà," said Kale, admiring their handiwork.

The Bland Sisters yawned. Exploring and thinking and planning and navigating were draining endeavors, especially when one does not perform those tasks regularly.

"It's late. Should we sleep here?" Kale asked.

"The deck's too hard," Jaundice said. "We need to find beds."

"I bet there are beds down below," Kale said.

"Possibly," said Jaundice. "But we'll need to find a ladder that goes *down*."

The Bland Sisters were about to address this predicament when a bright light shone in their faces.

"W-who's there?" a timid voice said. It was Millie Mudd, one of the youngest of the crew, assigned as a lookout.

Jaundice decided to improvise. "Er, it's just Jaundice and Kale Bland, getting some fresh air. Kale's a bit seasick, unfortunately. She hasn't got her sea legs yet. Or her sea stomach."

In the light of Millie's lantern, Kale immediately began to look green and ill at ease. It was a bravura performance, Jaundice thought. Perhaps her sister had some marketable skills after all.

Millie Mudd sighed and lowered her lantern. "Yer not allowed to be above deck after sundown," she said, trying to sound stern. "Get down below now and see if ye can't find a place to rest yer bones."

"Aye aye," said Jaundice, executing a salute. Millie sighed again and moved along.

"Ohhhhh," said Kale.

"I know," said Jaundice. "That was close. But you saved it with your seasick routine. Well done."

"It's no act," Kale said. "I think something in that stew didn't agree with me. Look out!"

And with that, Kale ran to the nearest railing, leaned over, and watched as her dinner jumped ship and floated away on the waves.

"Rats," she said, without a hint of irony.

paraphernalia |ˌparəfə(r)ˈnālyə| *noun*
equipment needed for a particular activity

←——— Chapter Twelve ———→

The Bland Sisters could not find any beds below deck, as the pirates of *The Jolly Regina* slept in hammocks. By the time Jaundice and Kale discovered this fact, there were no spare hammocks to be had, so they spent their first night aboard sprawled on two lumpy sacks of grain in the galley. As you might imagine, the night involved quite a bit of tossing and turning.

"This can't be good for my back," Jaundice said in the morning, stretching awkwardly. "Or my front."

"Is this burlap?" Kale said, poking at the sack. "I think I'm chafed again."

"I miss our cozy beds at home," said Jaundice. "The blankets, the sheets, the pillows . . ."

"The *mattresses*," Kale said, sighing.

As the sisters attempted to rouse themselves, they heard a terrible clatter, followed by a string of words Jaundice and Kale had never heard before, or seen in their dictionary— though they had a pretty good idea what they were.

"Profanities," Kale whispered to Jaundice.

"Obscenities," Jaundice whispered to Kale.

"Stowaways!" a voice shouted at both of them.

Suddenly, the Bland Sisters were face-to-face with the chantey singer from the previous evening. It was confirmed, then: This was the cook. She was a rather large woman with very ruddy skin, and she was sweating quite a bit. While Jaundice and Kale didn't say it aloud, they were both thinking the same thing: The cook very much resembled a ham with a head on top.

For a ham with a head on top, she was strong. She grabbed Kale and Jaundice by their collars and held them aloft, their feet dangling well above the galley floor.

"Do ye know what we does to stowaways on *The Jolly Regina*?" the cook asked, her nostrils flaring.

"Um . . . the Jack Ketch?" suggested Kale.

"A sound keelhauling?" offered Jaundice.

"Or perhaps," guessed Kale, "a good marooning?"

"Hmm," the cook said, looking each of the sisters in the eye. "Yer awfully familiar with pirate justice."

"That's because we're not stowaways," said Kale.

"No?" said the cook.

"No," said Jaundice, looking around for an idea and seeing nothing but pots and pans and other kitcheny paraphernalia. She was stumped.

"We're, uh, we're here to assist *you*!" Kale exclaimed, finally.

"To assist *me*?" The cook threw her head back and laughed.

Jaundice glared at her sister, who gave her a little shrug. This situation had a good chance of going sour at any moment. After all, what did the Bland Sisters know about cooking, let alone pirate cooking? Dr. Snoote didn't feature any recipes, though he did offer a helpful Educational Sidebar called *How to Set a Table*.

"Well, well, well," the cook said. "It's about time they brought someone in to give old Fatima a hand. And two galley rats, no less! Though the two of ye together don't come close to measurin' up to me."

This was true, on many levels.

Fatima let go of Jaundice and Kale, who stumbled to the floor. "Well? What are ye waiting for? An in-vee-tation? Grab those sacks ye were lazin' on and help me with breakfast!"

How to Set a Table

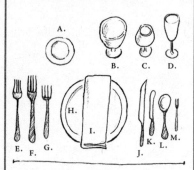

❧ Formal table setting ❧

A · BREAD PLATE

B · WATER GLASS

C · WINE GLASS

D · CHAMPAGNE GLASS

E · FORK (FISH)

F · FORK (DINNER)

G · FORK (SALAD)

H · PLATE

I · NAPKIN

J · DINNER KNIFE

K · FISH KNIFE

L · SOUP SPOON

M · OYSTER FORK

As it turned out, each of the grain sacks weighed more than each of the sisters, so it took both of them using all their strength to lift each one. Fatima pulled away the cauldron filled with stew and replaced it on the hearth with an empty pot. She lifted the cauldron lid and smiled at the contents.

"This seemed to go over well with the girls last night, eh?" she said. "No one says no to a bowl of Fatima's Finest."

Kale felt a rising of bile in the back of her throat. She tried not to look directly at the stew that had plagued her so terribly the night before, which was wise, as it appeared even less appetizing by the light of day.

"So what are you making?" asked Jaundice.

"*We're* makin' what the girls like every mornin'," the cook said, unfolding a long, sharp jackknife. The Bland Sisters' eyes grew wide as the blade flashed before them and sliced open the sacks of grain. "Fatima's Rib-Stickin' Gruel."

Kale leafed through the G section of her dictionary while Jaundice looked inside the sacks. The contents were familiar. In fact, they'd seen the very same contents in their sundries basket each week.

"Oats," Jaundice said.

"Yep," said Kale, showing her sister Dr. Snoote's definition. "Gruel is oatmeal."

"I don't care what fancy names ye have fer it," Fatima growled, pointing the knife at them. "Fatima calls it *gruel!*"

"Of course. My mistake," Kale said, as Fatima lowered the blade. She indicated the basket filled with hard crackers. "And what are these, then?"

"What? Are ye *addled*? Everyone knows that be hardtack biscuits," the cook said, taking the top off of one of the barrels. It was filled with water. She pointed to it with a sausagey finger. "Now, scoop that into the pot until it's half full." Then she handed a bucket to Jaundice. "And you, go down to Lizzie in the hold and get this filled with milk."

Kale and Jaundice did what they were told. Though in their minds, they knew they were making oatmeal, and this pleased them to no end. Of all the things in the world pirates liked to eat for breakfast, it was the very thing the Bland Sisters ate each morning, too.

negligence |ˈneglǝjǝns| *noun*
failure to take enough care

Chapter Thirteen.

Of course, Jaundice took a bit of a detour on her way to find Lizzie and the milk. She climbed up to the deck and waited until Millie Mudd was at the other end of the ship, then she rerouted the *Regina* to sail south.

"Easy cheesy," Jaundice whispered under her breath. Following a plan was almost as satisfying as following their daily routine at home. Jaundice missed their routine; doing the same things over and over again each day helped pass the time, and kept the Bland Sisters' hands and minds occupied.

It was Jaundice who had come up with the idea for the sock-darning business. She wrote up the sign that said:

SOCKS DARNED BY BLAND SISTERS.

TWO DOLLARS PER SOCK. THREE DOLLARS PER PAIR.

DEPOSIT MENDABLES AND PAYMENTS
AND PICK UP DARNED SOCKS IN BASKET
AT DULLSVILLE GROCERY.

NO SOCK TURNED AWAY.

Thankfully, the grocery was open to trafficking the
darning basket along with the sundries basket. Until they were
kidnapped by pirates, the Bland Sisters were doing a decent
business, Jaundice recalled. As she was good at numbers, she
also handled the money.

Now she just needed to find this Lizzie person who knew
where the milk was kept. Unfortunately, she couldn't seem
to find anyone down in the hold, it was filled with so many
animals: chickens, pigs, goats, and a cow.

"Hello?" Jaundice called. "Lizzie? Are you here?"

The cow behind Jaundice mooed softly.

"Shh," said Jaundice, stroking the cow's nose. "I'm trying to find someone."

Again and again, she called Lizzie's name, walking all around the hold, with no luck. Jaundice leaned against the cow's pen and sighed. Clearly, this woman was not where she

was supposed to be. Jaundice had half a mind to report her for negligence.

"And look," Jaundice said, pointing at the rail of the pen. "Lizzie's even carved her name here, so I know she must be skulking around somewhere."

Moooooooo, said the cow, gazing at Jaundice with her big, dark eyes.

Jaundice looked at the name carved on the rail.

She looked at the cow.

"Lizzie?" she said.

The cow blinked.

Jaundice blinked back.

"Ah," she said. "Well, then."

bereft |biˈreft| *adjective*
lacking in something
needed, expected, or desired

Chapter Fourteen

While Jaundice was gone, Kale was feeling a bit bereft. Somehow, she'd learned to live without her parents, but she'd never been apart from her sister, ever. And Fatima was not working out as a substitute.

"Stop watching the pot, galley rat!" she shouted from her stool. "It'll never boil!"

But Kale enjoyed watching the pot. It reminded her of their oatmeal pot at home, only this one was about ten times as big, and at least ten times as dirty. Clearly, Fatima needed some help in the housekeeping department. Kale looked around at the rest of the galley, which was equally filthy.

"I think I'll tidy up a bit," Kale announced, grabbing a broom.

"Suit yerself," grumbled Fatima.

At home, Kale found great satisfaction in cleaning. At first, it was because she wanted to keep the house in order for her mother and father, for whenever they returned from their unspecified errand. When it became clear that they were not coming back any time soon, cleaning became less a series of tasks for Kale and more an all-consuming passion. She would spend hours polishing a single spoon or cheese knife to gleaming perfection, and devoted her every weekend to washing windows, vacuuming carpets, dusting knickknacks, and her favorite domestic chore of all: scouring the bathroom sink, bathtub, and toilet, which she found was best accomplished with her favorite cleaning implement, a toothbrush. (It might be helpful to clarify that Kale was in the habit of cleaning with an *old* toothbrush, and not one in current use for the cleaning of her teeth or Jaundice's.) The best part about cleaning, for Kale, at least, was that it was never done. Sooner or later, everything would get dirty again, and she would happily start over with her regimen.

"So," said Kale, sweeping the floor one plank at a time, "how long have you been a pirate?"

"Oh, it's been close to ten years now," Fatima said, cleaning her fingernails with her knife. "But I been a cook fer half that time. Ever since the accident."

"The accident?" Kale asked. She stopped sweeping and gave the cook her full attention. This had the potential of being another story.

"I used to be the lookout here on the *Regina*, but they've got that Millie Mudd doin' it now," the cook began. "I could spot land a day away, without even usin' a spyglass."

"And then what?" Kale prodded.

Fatima sighed. "Well, weren't much to do up there in the crow's nest, other than look out fer land and other ships, and eat hardtack. Ye can see where that got me: a bit broad in the beam, and not in the best of shapes."

This was true. Fatima was nothing if not spherical.

"So one day I'm up there, and I spy a ship we've been tryin' to track down: *The Booty Myth*, captained by the fugitive Ann Tennille. I jump up to give Delilah the 'Sail ho,' and me feet crash through the bottom of the crow's nest. Next thing I know, I'm flat on me back on the deck, starin' at the sky."

"Gosh," said Kale. "Were you all right?"

"Nary a scratch on me," said Fatima. "Thankfully, I had somethin' to cushion me bum."

"A bag of grain? A coil of rope? A folded-up bit of sailcloth?" Kale guessed.

"Nah," said Fatima. "'Twas Peg."

"Oh, dear," said Kale.

"She never knew what hit her," said Fatima. "Until she woke up and someone told her. She was fine, except fer her leg. Though that was nothin' that a jug o' rum and a sure blade couldn't fix."

Kale tried not to visualize the details. "Wasn't she upset? About losing her leg?"

"Not so much as you'd think," said Fatima. "She said she never liked that leg much, anyway. And she forgave me fer my part in the whole incident, bless her one-legged heart. That's a true friend, see. Someone who'll always be there fer ye. Even to break yer fall."

"So how did you end up in the galley?" Kale asked.

"Guess Delilah and Lefty felt it suited me. I'm too big fer much else these days, anyway," Fatima said, sighing. "Such a stereotype, that is: Make the chunky one a cook. But I try not to let it take the wind out of me sails. Like I always say, When Life Gives Ye Rats, Make Stew."

Kale didn't have time to ponder the implications of Fatima's adage, as their conversation was interrupted by the return of her sister. Jaundice looked a bit worse for wear. Her clothes and hair were soaked, and she had the distinct markings of hoofprints on her shirtfront.

"I've got the milk," she said weakly, holding out the pail.

"It's about time, shark bait," Fatima growled. She grabbed the milk and began stirring it into the pot of pasty oats. Jaundice climbed onto the nearest stool, put her head down on the table, and thought wistfully of how easily milk was procured by the Bland Sisters before today, delivered in clean glass bottles to their basket by the mailbox.

Kale patted her sister on the shoulder.

"Cow milking must be a trying endeavor," she whispered.

"Utterly," said Jaundice. Though "udderly" might have been more apt.

vehemence |ˈvēəməns| *noun*
force, intensity, or passion

Chapter Fifteen

After another few minutes of stirring, Fatima decided that the gruel was ready.

"You!" she yelled at Jaundice. "Grab them bowls!"

"You!" she yelled at Kale. "Grab them spoons and tankards!"

The Bland Sisters did what they were told, with concerted effort. The bowls and spoons and tankards were made of wood and they weighed a great deal. Fatima, however, had no trouble. With one arm, she picked up the gigantic pot of gruel as if it weighed nothing, then lifted a keg of ale and put it under her other arm. Jaundice and Kale took simultaneous note of this; also, they made a note never to get on Fatima's bad side, more than they already had, anyway.

The crew was assembled in the hold just below deck. They were evidently very hungry and not in possession of very good manners; everyone was pounding on the table in unison, shouting, "Food! Now! Food! Now! Food! Now!"

"All right, all right," Fatima shouted back, seemingly louder than all the other voices rolled into one. The Bland Sisters were impressed; she had not only exceptional upper arm strength, but also a sizable pair of lungs and a remarkable ability to project her voice. Fatima brought the pot of gruel down on the table with a *THUNK*. Then she motioned to Kale and Jaundice. "What ye waitin' fer, bilge suckers? Start servin'!"

The Bland Sisters hurried around the table, setting out bowls and spoons and tankards. It turned out Dr. Snoote's table-setting guide really did come in handy.

"Got yerself some lackeys, I see, Fatty," said a pirate named Princess. She was tall and very thin, and covered nearly head to toe in tattoos, except for her teeth, which were studded with diamonds.

"I need *someone* to do me dirty work," Fatima replied, plopping gruel into Princess's bowl. "Not like any of ye wenches were volunteerin'."

"I didn't think anyone else could fit in that galley with ye," Princess said. "Not with the ballast *yer* carrying."

"Ye lassies best be careful," a pirate named Smokey said to Kale and Jaundice, puffing on a mermaid-shaped pipe. "Ole Fatty here might run out of hardtack and eat ye both as a snack."

Just about everyone at the table laughed, even Fatima herself. Though the Bland Sisters could tell that the cook was only pretending to think the jokes were funny, as she gritted her teeth and plopped gruel into Princess's and Smokey's bowls with particular vehemence.

"Come on, now, mateys. That's enough humor fer one mornin'," Peg said, giving Fatima a sympathetic look.

"Good ole Fatty," Smokey said through a spoonful of gruel. "She knows how to take a ribbin'."

"She's got a thick skin, that one. A *very* thick skin," said Princess. The crew erupted into laughter again.

Making fun of other people's appearances isn't nice, Jaundice and Kale thought at the same time, as they filled the pirates' tankards with ale. But, as they came to realize, most pirates aren't very nice, either.

tact |takt| *noun*
the ability to deal with
others or with difficult
issues without offense

<hr />

Chapter Sixteen

S o why is she called 'Princess'?" Kale asked after breakfast.
She was thoroughly scrubbing the bowls, spoons,
tankards, and gruel pot, Jaundice was drying and stacking,
and Fatima was supervising, which meant she was sitting on a
stool, eating a considerable amount of hardtack.

"Her full name is Princess Kwee-Kweg," Fatima grumbled
between bites. Crumbs of hardtack quivered on her chin as
she spoke. "But most of the crew has trouble with pro-nun-see-
a-tin', so we all just calls her Princess. She claims to be royalty,
from some place."

"A real princess," said Jaundice, who had only ever seen one princess, as illustrated in their dictionary. "I can't believe it."

"Her tattoos are incredible," said Kale, who had only ever seen one tattoo, as illustrated in their dictionary. "They must have taken forever to apply. And I bet they were painful, especially in, you know, the more sensitive areas."

"Like her toes," added Jaundice.

Jaundice had particularly sensitive toes. She didn't like having them touched, even a little bit. All in good fun, Kale once brushed her sister's big toe with the tip of a feather; Jaundice wouldn't speak to her for days. She rarely ever went barefoot and preferred wearing socks to bed, even in the summer, all to prevent her toes from potentially brushing up against anything. This was merely one of many quirks maintained by the Bland Sisters, as one may have already surmised.

"The more painful for Princess, the better," Fatima mumbled, reaching for another biscuit. "An' I can suggest a few sensitive areas that Smokey should think about tattooin'."

"Do you have any cheese?" Jaundice asked. "Those biscuits would taste better with some cheese, I bet."

"These biscuits taste just fine. Mind yer own business," Fatima snapped, turning away.

Even with Fatima's back turned, it soon became clear to

the Bland Sisters that she was crying. Her whole body shook with the eruption of tears, which made the pots and pans around her begin to clatter. Jaundice and Kale looked at each other. It was the first time they had ever seen such an emotional display; it all seemed so wet and troubling. This was a situation in need of considerable delicacy and tact, neither of which the Bland Sisters had any practice in exercising.

"You know," said Kale, "we don't think you're fat at all."

Unfortunately, this made Fatima cry even harder. Kale looked at her sister for assistance. Jaundice cleared her throat.

"No," Jaundice added. "You're very sturdy. And strong. *Very* strong. We're considerably impressed with the way you carry the gruel pot and the ale keg. No one else on the crew could even attempt such a feat."

"And," said Kale, "you can carry a tune. We heard you singing your chantey last night. It was delightful."

"I can't tell you how much I enjoyed it," said Jaundice. Which was, in its own way, the truth.

"Really?" Fatima sniffed. "I wrote that, ye know."

"You did?" Kale said, with genuine incredulity. "I've never heard anything like it in all my life."

This was true; as was previously mentioned, the Bland Sisters couldn't remember hearing any song before, let alone a chantey, let alone a chantey performed live by a pirate of certain girth while doing a jig.

"*But why do they always have to make fun of me?*" Fatima cried, burying her face in her apron.

"It's because you're special, obviously," Jaundice said gently. "They're just jealous."

"Also," Kale added, "from what little I've seen, people make themselves feel better by being mean to others."

"That's true," Fatima said, sniffing. "That's what I do. I'm mean to everyone I meet. Why, I've been a right old crab to ye two, and ye've been nothing but nice to me."

"And patient," added Jaundice.

"And helpful," Kale reminded, gesturing around the galley. It really was much cleaner.

Fatima dried her eyes with her stained apron. She put her arms around the Bland Sisters. "Ye girls are good to ole Fatima," she said, pulling them in close. "I'm glad I have ye. And Peg."

If she squeezed any tighter, Fatima wouldn't have either of the Bland Sisters much longer. Fortunately, Lefty appeared in the galley doorway. Fatima loosened her headlocks and Jaundice and Kale breathed sighs of relief. They weren't used to giving or receiving hugs, especially of the extreme variety.

"How are these bilge rats working out?" Lefty asked, looking around. She slapped her cat-o'-nine-tails absentmindedly against her leg, which did not do much to help the Bland Sisters' nerves.

"Top-notch," Fatima said. "These lassies are keepers."

"Good," said Lefty, "because I need 'em for some hard scrubbin'. I want the decks lookin' as shipshape as this galley."

"But—but they just got here," said Fatima.

"Don't worry," Lefty said. "They'll be back in time to help ye make dinner."

As the Bland Sisters were led away, they made sure to wave to Fatima, as she was looking rather bereft. Kale, having felt the same way a mere few hours before, could fully empathize.

"Nice work," Jaundice whispered to her sister on the way out. "Now we have two jobs."

"But aren't two jobs better than one?" Kale asked.

"It would be, if we were getting paid," Jaundice said.

"Oh," said Kale. "True."

serendipity |ˌserənˈdipitē| *noun*
    a chance occurrence or development
    of events, leading to something
    delightful or valuable

Chapter Seventeen

And so, the Bland Sisters performed another several hours of hard scrubbing. The sun was so hot that Jaundice was almost tempted to remove her socks—almost. She wiped the sweat from her brow and sighed.

"This is harder than milking a cow," she said. "And that's saying a lot."

"I'm not even enjoying myself, and I *love* cleaning," said Kale.

"Here," whispered Peg, passing them a jug.

"What is it?" asked Kale.

"It's ale," said Peg. "It'll quench yer thirst."

"We don't drink alcohol," noted Jaundice.

Kale nodded in agreement. "Right," she said. "Alcohol is for adults, and pirates."

"It's not that kind of ale," Peg explained. "It's *ginger* ale, me own special brew. Quenches yer thirst, and cures seasickness. The ginger settles the stomach."

"I'll give it a try, then," said Kale, whose stomach was still feeling unsettled from last night's stew. She took the jug from Peg, uncorked it, and gave it a sniff. She had never smelled ginger before, but found it not at all unpleasant. She looked at Jaundice, who shrugged. Kale took a sip.

"Mmm. Tastes like our soda at home," she said, burping softly. "Only not quite as flat."

Jaundice took a sip, too. "You're right. It does," she noted.

By this point in the afternoon, Deadeye Delilah had joined the rest of the crew on deck. She looked a bit worse for wear, most likely from consuming too much rum the evening before. She reclined in a chair with her scarf tied low over her eye and eye patch, flipping a shiny gold doubloon between her fingers, while Lefty steered the ship and watched over the crew. Scurvy seemed a bit more fully recuperated, and was scurrying around the deck, biting everyone's ankles and chattering. Peg gave him a good swat on the nose when he tried to approach her.

"I've a mind to toss that varmint overboard," she muttered.

"So," said Jaundice, "how long have you been a pirate?"

"Ohhh, close to five years now," said Peg. "It's a bit different from the library, I can tell ye. Much more water and much fewer books, that's fer sure."

"You were a librarian?" asked Kale.

"You don't look like a librarian," Jaundice noted. Of course, the only librarian the Bland Sisters had ever encountered was Dr. Snoote's illustration next to his definition of the term. It was a drawing of a serious-looking woman in a high-necked blouse with her hair in a bun. She carried an armful of books, and her index finger was raised to her lips, as if to say, "Shh!"

LIBRARIAN

"I presided over the main branch in Port Innastorm," Peg explained, dipping her scrub brush into the grungy pail of seawater. She had no trouble scrubbing as she talked.

"Aren't libraries a bit of a waste?" asked Kale. "I mean, why do you need so many books when you can just have a dictionary? Dr. Snoote tells us everything about everything."

"Dictionaries are just words and meanings. Dry as sand," Peg answered. "Books are filled with adventures and emotions and ideas!"

Kale blinked. She and Jaundice had been living without those things for as long as she could remember. And they were perfectly fine. Weren't they?

"For years, I did it all: shelved the books, kept track of the returns, helped the patrons find what they needed," Peg continued. "But ye know what?"

"What?" said Kale. She rested her head on her hands. She was getting a Feeling. A someone's-about-to-tell-a-story Feeling.

"After bein' around all them books about foreign places and people and things, I wanted to see 'em for meself. I wanted to discover the stories behind the stories. Know what I mean?"

The Bland Sisters nodded, though they had no idea what Peg meant. Kale held her dictionary to her chest. She couldn't imagine a life without Dr. Snoote.

"So one mornin', I locked up the library," Peg continued, "and I walked down to the dock and volunteered for the first ship I saw. Which just happened to be this one. I got lucky, I did."

"But if you didn't become a pirate on *The Jolly Regina*, you wouldn't have lost your leg," Kale reminded her.

"I also wouldn't have met Fatima," Peg replied. "I lost me leg and found a best friend, all at once. That was serendipity, that was. And ye never turn down a moment of serendipity. Eventually, no matter how bad things are, it all leads to somethin'—or someone—worth all the trouble."

The Bland Sisters pondered this theory with more than a little suspicion. It didn't seem possible that everything bad eventually leads to something good. Perhaps, Jaundice and Kale decided, Peg suffered a blow to the head as well as the leg when Fatima fell on her.

"Did you see our parents when they were here on the ship?" Jaundice asked, hoping to change the subject.

Peg was about to respond when Delilah's voice bellowed from her hammock.

"Whoever's talkin', SHUT YER TRAPS!" she groaned. "I've got a HEED-ache!"

Lefty glared in the direction of Peg and the Bland Sisters. She took out her cat-o'-nine-tails and slapped it against the palm of her hand a few times. Then she went back to looking at her maps.

"I seen yer ma an' pop," Peg whispered. "They was on

board the *Regina* fer three days, though Delilah had 'em locked in the brig the whole time, cuz they wouldn't tell her where Captain Ann's treasure was hidden. Not at first, anyway."

"Our parents were prisoners?" Kale said.

"So what were they like?" Jaundice asked.

"Quite a pair, those two," Peg said. "Yer ma taught me to play three new tunes on the hornpipe, and within three days, she could imitate just about everyone in the crew. And yer pop could tell the same joke in seven different languages, all of 'em just as funny. A breath of fresh air, they were. Too bad they were marooned—we was all sorry to see 'em go."

With that, Peg went along scrubbing. The Bland Sisters followed suit, working side by side.

"I wish I remembered our parents," Jaundice whispered to her sister.

"The more I try, the more I think I might miss them," admitted Kale.

For the remainder of the afternoon, the Bland Sisters continued their labor. The scrubbing didn't seem quite as difficult now, as they both daydreamed about their mother's musicality and imitations and their father's proficiency with languages and joke telling. Already, they sounded like fascinating people. More fascinating than Jaundice or Kale, anyway.

Of course, as you've learned by now, that's not saying much.

vicious circle |ˌvɪʃəs ˌsərkəl| *noun*
a repeating and worsening situation

Chapter Eighteen

As Lefty promised, the Bland Sisters were returned to Fatima in time to prepare the evening meal. Thankfully, the meal was leftover stew from the night before, which involved very little preparation (or cow milking). Kale was grateful to Jaundice for volunteering to prepare and serve the stew, while Kale was left to dispense the far-less-nauseating hardtack.

"We'll just add a little water to the pot, to loosen things up a bit," Fatima said. "Stew tends to get a bit pasty by day two."

The Bland Sisters wrinkled their noses. By the look and smell of it, Fatima had confused *pasty* with *rancid*.

"So where's the hardtack?" Kale asked, looking around the table. "There was a whole bushel of biscuits here this morning."

"Oh, I polished them off hours ago," Fatima said, looking a bit sheepish.

"All of them?" Kale said. She held up the bushel, and turned it over. Not even a crumb remained. "But there were *dozens* in here. You mean to say you ate them *all?*"

"So what if I did?" Fatima snapped. "I was anxious. When I'm anxious, me gullet gets gnashy."

The Bland Sisters realized that Fatima was caught in a bit of a vicious circle: The more she ate, the more the other pirates made fun of her. And the more the other pirates made fun of her, the more she ate.

"Maybe you need to find something else to do when you feel anxious," Kale said. "Otherwise, you're going to give yourself a stomachache."

"And we're going to run out of hardtack altogether," Jaundice added.

"Like what?" Fatima asked. "What else could I do, other than stuff me face?"

"Give me a moment," said Kale, closing her eyes. She had never felt anxious, so she never had to distract herself. Perhaps this was because she was always doing things she enjoyed: staring at wallpaper, watching grass grow, eating oatmeal or cheese sandwiches, reading the dictionary with Jaundice, etc., etc. If only Fatima had something she enjoyed as much as eating.

Ah, thought Kale, opening her eyes. That's it.

"Do you still have that crumpled napkin in your smock pocket?" she asked Jaundice. "And that burned stick?"

Of course, Jaundice did. Kale spread the napkin on the table. She handed the stick to Fatima.

"Okay," said Kale. "Jaundice is going to add water to the stew and cook up some more hardtack. And you and I are going to write a new chantey."

"I am?" said Jaundice.

"We are?" said Fatima.

"From what I've heard, musicality runs in our family," Kale assured the cook. Then she turned to her sister. "And you're not the only one who gets to have a plan."

As it was the first plan Kale ever devised, it wasn't much, really: just something to write with and write on and a bit of determination. Though, sometimes, that's more than enough.

scrimshaw |ˈskrimˌshô| *noun*
a carved or engraved item, usually
made from whalebone, ivory, or shell

— Chapter Nineteen —

Food! Now! Food! Now! Food! Now!"

And so it went, with everyone in the crew chanting and pounding on the table. It really was quite rude. The Bland Sisters were glad they'd soon be leaving the ship and reunited with their parents, as they'd just about had their fill of this poor pirate etiquette.

Fatima was clearly anxious, as her foul temper had returned in full force.

"You!" she yelled at Jaundice. "Hand out them bowls!"

"You!" she yelled at Kale. "Hand out them spoons and tankards!"

"Easy, now. Remember our plan," Kale whispered.

Fatima forced her mouth into a smile. She began walking between the tables, doling out the stew with a big iron ladle. Kale followed behind, giving each pirate one of Jaundice's hardtack biscuits. Somehow, Jaundice found a way to make the hardtack taste stale from the moment it came off the hearth. Baking was not one of her special talents, though the crew of the *Regina* didn't seem to mind, or even notice.

"Wide load, comin' through!" Princess called as Fatima brushed past her. The rest of the crew erupted into laughter, except for Fatima, and the Bland Sisters, and Peg.

Smokey puffed on her pipe. "I haven't seen a bum that big since we had that African elephant on board," she said loudly, inciting further hysterics.

And so it went. Princess and Smokey continued their remarks all through dinner, as if they were performing a stand-up routine for the rest of the crew. Fatima sat at the other end of the table, looking down at her bowl. She didn't take a single bite of stew.

"You're not eating?" Jaundice said, attempting to chew a bite of hardtack.

"I think I lost me appetite," Fatima whispered.

"You said 'no one can say no to Fatima's Finest,'" Kale said, patting the cook on the arm. "Besides, you have to keep your energy up for later."

Fatima took a few tentative bites as Kale and Jaundice filled Peg in on the plan. Peg went down to the crew's quarters after dinner to get her hornpipe. When she returned, she gave a nod to Jaundice, who gave Kale a nudge. Kale climbed up on a keg of ale and cleared her throat.

"Ahem," she said. "Now that you've all enjoyed a bowl of Fatima's Finest, it's time you enjoyed an earful of song from the cook herself. Friends, sisters, and pirates, *The Jolly Regina* is proud to present the musical stylings of none other than . . . Fatima!"

Everyone in the crew began clapping. Lefty put her fingers in her mouth and let out a long whistle. Fatima rose, slowly, and stood next to Peg.

"Thar she blows!" Smokey shouted.

"Careful, Peg!" Princess added. "Ye don't want to lose the other leg!"

Of course, everyone laughed at this. Peg gave her friend a pat on the shoulder, then blew a few opening notes on her hornpipe. Fatima looked out into the crowd, then back at the Bland Sisters and Peg.

"Here goes nothin'," she muttered.

She took a deep breath. Then she opened her mouth and began singing.

Ohh ye calls me big ole Fatty
and ye makes fun of me girth;
I've endured more defamation
than anyone on earth.

I likes to eat me hardtack,
I likes to drink me ale,
but that don't mean I likes to be
com-pa-red to a whale.

At this point, the Bland Sisters chimed in with the chorus:

Yo-ho-ho! Fatty-o!
Yo-ho-ho! Fatty-go!
Yo-ho-ho! Fatty-o!
Yo-ho-ho! Fatty-go!

The crew pounded their tankards against the table to the beat. Peg was tapping her wooden leg, and the Bland Sisters were clapping. Feeling encouraged, Fatima seemed a bit bolder now.

"Are ye ready for the second verse?" she bellowed.

The crew whooped and hollered in affirmation.

"Well, all right then. Hold on to yer booty, cuz here we

go," Fatima said, squeezing in right behind Princess and Smokey as she started in again.

I'll never be a pretty Princess
with skin covered with ink;
pity she don't bathe more often—
she makes a royal stink!

I'll never be like Smokey,
so quick to quip and snipe;
I'll never tell her where to stick
her pretty ivory pipe!

Yo-ho-ho! Fatty-o!
Yo-ho-ho! Fatty-go!
Yo-ho-ho! Fatty-o!
Yo-ho-ho! Fatty-go!

"You tell 'em, Fatty!" Lefty shouted. Fatima curtsied in response.

Everyone in the crew joined the Bland Sisters in the chorus that time, except for Princess and Smokey, of course. They both looked as if they'd swallowed a tough bite of hardtack.

Fatima stood by the end of the table now, her foot up on the bench. The crew was in stitches.

"All right, all right," Fatima called. "Time for the big finish, then. Ready?"

If ye thinks me song is hurtful,
if ye thinks ye've been maligned,
just remember how ye've treated me
and how ye've been unkind.

And remember—I can exercise,
I can change the shape I'm in,
but no matter what ye wenches do
ye'll still be ugly as sin!

Yo-ho-ho! Fatty-o!
Yo-ho-ho! Fatty-go!
Yo-ho-ho! Fatty-o!
Yo-ho-ho!
Fatty!
GO!

At the last note, Fatima brought her foot down hard on the bench. It flipped up in the air, taking Princess and Smokey along with it. They slid into the ale keg and landed in a heap as the rest of the crew fell into near convulsions of laughter.

"Whoopsie," Fatima said. "Guess I don't know me own strength."

"Look!" said Kale.

The ale keg had burst, drenching Princess and Smokey. Princess was covered in what looked like black smudges. Her tattoos had dissolved.

"Oh!" she cried, looking down at herself. "I thought I used waterproof ink!"

"It's the ale, dummy," Peg noted. "That stuff will cut through anythin'. That's why I brew me own."

It was true; the pirates used the ale not only for drinking, but also for cleaning the barnacles from the sides of the ship and removing particularly set-in stains.

"Fake teeth *and* fake tattoos? Is she even actually a princess?" Jaundice asked.

"Nah, she's a barmaid from Port Innastorm. Her real name's Doris," Smokey grumbled, crawling around on her hands and knees. "Has anyone seen me mermaid pipe?"

"That was supposed to be a secret! You promised not to tell!" Doris said, covering her ink-smeared face with her hands and bursting into tears.

"Is this it?" Kale asked. She held up the black mouthpiece of the pipe. The mermaid had broken off, leaving a jagged bit of ivory at one end.

Smokey growled and advanced toward Kale, brandishing a rather sharp-looking switchblade. "That mermaid was a one-of-a-kind scrimshaw," she said. "I should know—I killed the guy who made it. With this knife, in fact."

"I didn't break it," Kale said meekly. "I just *found* it."

"Ye did her a favor, anyways," said Fatima. "Smokin' is a filthy habit."

But Smokey wasn't in the mood to listen. "Gaaaah!" she shouted, lunging at Kale.

Fortunately, Peg held out her wooden leg at just the right moment. The knife plunged into it with a loud *THONK*.

"See?" Peg said, holding up her leg for all to see. "Serendipity. That's what that is. If this was me real leg, we'd have a not-so-happy resolution, wouldn't we?"

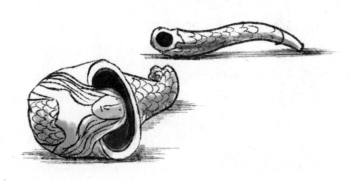

saboteurs |ˌsabəˈtərs| *plural noun*
people who deliberately destroy
or damage something

<hr />

←——— Chapter Twenty ———→

The Bland Sisters were feeling rather pleased with themselves. Though they'd barely set foot outside their little house before now, they'd secretly and cleverly navigated *The Jolly Regina* to sail in the direction of Gilly Guns Island, where they would soon surprise their parents with a heroic rescue. They led Fatima to exact some very satisfying poetic justice and find newfound confidence as a chanteuse and reformed binge eater. They watched as Smokey and The Pirate Formerly Known as Princess were taken to the brig by Lefty, where they were to remain for a week for assaulting a fellow crew member with a knife, and for misrepresenting oneself

as royalty, respectively. And with those two pirates gone, they finally found a place to sleep in the crew's quarters, and discovered that hammocks are not altogether uncomfortable for sleeping. All in all, it was turning out to be a fairly positive experience, this pirate kidnapping. Perhaps it was a case of serendipity after all.

Or not.

In the morning, Jaundice and Kale rose early and went on deck to realign the ship's wheel for the last time.

"I bet we'll be there by nightfall," Jaundice said.

"And then what?" asked Kale.

"What do you mean, 'and then what'?" asked Jaundice.

"I mean, how are we going to get from *The Jolly Regina* to the island without being caught, and how are we going to get our parents off the island once we find them?" Kale explained.

"Hmm." Jaundice shoved her hands in her smock pockets, and took a moment to ponder this. Think! Think! she thought to herself. She'd never had to make a plan before, so she was a bit sketchy on the follow-through. Honestly, she had never thought beyond the resteering of the ship. The rescue warranted another round of plan making altogether.

Unfortunately, Jaundice's thought process was interrupted by the sound of a monkey. Scurvy's screeching had an exceptionally shrill quality, which made both sisters cover their ears and squeeze their eyes shut until the noise subsided. When they finally opened their eyes, they were surrounded by the entire crew, including Lefty and Deadeye Delilah. Delilah looked even worse than she had the day before; clearly, she needed to stay away from the rum.

"What's this?" she said, examining the scene. "Scurvy knows not to wake me before noon, unless it's an emergency."

"The wheel! It's been moved!" Lefty cried. Jaundice had been too busy thinking about the next step of her plan to realign the wheel for the last time. The ship was still headed west.

Immediately, Scurvy leaped onto Jaundice and perched on her head. He began pointing at both Bland Sisters and continued screeching, no matter how much they swatted at him.

"You don't say?" Delilah responded, nodding at the monkey, then turning to Lefty. "He says these two is the

perpetrators. I knew I shouldn't have trusted 'em, not after dealin' with their shifty parents."

The Bland Sisters attempted to appear innocent and indignant. Soon, Fatima and Peg pushed through the crowd.

"Yer takin' the word of Scurvy over these lassies?" Fatima said to the captain and first mate.

"They've done nothin' but good for this ship since they got here," Peg added.

Delilah shrugged. "I never doubt me monkey," she said.

Lefty leaned in close to the Bland Sisters, close enough for them to smell last night's stew on her breath. Kale felt the bile rise in her throat.

"Ye know what we does to saboteurs?" Lefty growled.

"Do we get a choice?" Jaundice pleaded. "Because I'd prefer *anything* but being marooned on Gilly Guns Island."

At this, she winked at her sister. Kale was quick to catch on.

"Right," she said. "Do anything you want to us. Just *please* . . . not Gilly Guns Island!"

Lefty and Delilah looked at the Bland Sisters, then at each other. Then they started laughing. Jaundice and Kale started laughing, too, though they had no idea what was so funny.

Delilah's mood suddenly grew serious. She leaned in close to the Bland Sisters as well. Her rummy breath was almost as bad as Lefty's.

"Do ye think we're addle brained?" she said. "Do ye *really* think we'd maroon ye on the same island where we dumped yer parents so ye can all have a happy family reunion?"

"I think these two should get a sound keelhaulin', *Regina*-style," Lefty said.

"Ohhh, now don't that sound delightful?" Delilah said. "We haven't had a keelhaul here fer *ages*."

Scurvy jumped on Delilah's shoulder and squealed in approval.

"Um, what's a keelhaul again?" asked Jaundice.

"It's not in here *anywhere*," said Kale, consulting Dr. Snoote.

"We ties a rope to ye, then we tosses ye overboard and let ye drag underwater until ye drown, or get chopped up by barnacles, or both," Delilah informed them, rubbing her hands together with glee. "Stick *that* in yer dictionary."

"But what makes it *really* special is the way we does it here on the *Regina*," Lefty said, grabbing two coils of rope.

"And . . . how's that?" Kale asked, gulping.

"We ties the rope to yer toes," Delilah said happily.

At this point, a loud *THUD* could be heard on deck. It was the sound of Jaundice slipping to the floor in a dead faint. Though it was the first time she ever fainted, it was perfectly executed.

steadfast |ˈstedˌfast| *adjective*
firm and unwavering

— Chapter Twenty-one —

By the time Jaundice awoke, the damage had already been done; a rope was securely affixed to her toes. Kale faced an identical situation, though she was merely terrified. The feeling of the scratchy rope around her toes made Jaundice feel terrified *and* downright squeamish.

"Ohhhh," Jaundice groaned. "Noooo."

"Don't look at it," Kale whispered. "We've got other things to think about."

"Like . . . what?" Jaundice said, focusing on the seagulls overhead and trying not to hyperventilate.

"Let's think of a plan," Kale said, closing her eyes. She was

getting pretty good at this thinking business. "Maybe, once they throw us overboard, we can find a way to untie ourselves. And then we can swim until we find land. There must be land within swimming distance, in some direction."

"There's one problem," said Jaundice.

"What's that?" asked Kale.

"We don't know how to swim," said Jaundice.

"Excellent point," said Kale.

SNAP!

Lefty cracked her cat-o'-nine-tails, inspiring immediate and total silence.

"By the power vested in me as first mate of *The Jolly Regina*, I pronounce these two sisters guilty of the charge of sab-ee-tage," she announced to the crowd, "a crime carryin' a penalty of death by keelhaul, *Jolly Regina*-style, such sentence to commence immediately and without delay."

"Wait," Jaundice said. "Don't we even get a trial?"

"What do ye think we are here, civilized?" Delilah said, laughing. Scurvy, perched on her shoulder, laughed, too.

"But we were just trying to rescue our parents," Kale pleaded.

"Oh, me heart *bleeds* fer ye," Delilah said, clutching her chest melodramatically. "The first rule of piratin' is steadfast loyalty to yer ship and yer shipmates, above everythin'. Includin' yer bloomin' family. Am I right?"

Everyone on deck cheered in approval, except for Fatima and Peg. Fatima was crying, and Peg was consoling her.

"Those girls was good to me!" Fatima wailed. "And now they's gonna feed the fish!"

"I suppose this is the end for us, then," Kale said to Jaundice.

"Yes, well," Jaundice said, "you can't say we haven't lived a full life."

The Bland Sisters considered this. Briefly.

"At least we've had each other," Kale said.

"True," Jaundice said, closing her eyes, so as not to see the rope around her toe. "True."

Lefty grabbed hold of Jaundice and Delilah grabbed hold of Kale.

"On the count of three, we toss 'em," Lefty said.

"I want to do the countin' this time," Delilah said. "You *always* get to do the countin'."

Lefty sighed. "Fine, then."

Delilah cleared her throat. The Bland Sisters grabbed each other's hands tightly.

"One . . ." she said. "Two . . ."

"SAIL HO!" called a voice from above.

"That's not the way it's supposed to go," Lefty said.

"That wasn't me," Delilah said, looking up in the direction of the voice.

It was Millie Mudd, up in the crow's nest. She'd taken off her bandanna and was waving it to get everyone's attention.

"SAIL HO!" she called again, pointing. "SAIL HO!"

Everyone turned to see where she was pointing, including the Bland Sisters, who were happy to get a reprieve, if only briefly.

"A ship?" Lefty said.

Delilah pulled out her spyglass to get a look. Her mouth fell open.

"It's not just any ship, me hearty," she said. "It's *The Booty Myth*!"

swashbuckling |ˈswôshˌbəkling| *noun*
brave and daring adventures, usually
conducted with flamboyance

— Chapter Twenty-two —

*T*he *Booty Myth*, it turned out, was a faster ship than *The
Jolly Regina*. Much faster. Within minutes, the vessels
were within a few yards of each other. The Bland Sisters could
see a tall woman with long red hair standing on the bow,
dressed all in white and gold, from her tricorn hat to her high,
laced-up boots. She was smiling.

"That must be Captain Ann," Jaundice whispered.

"I'm getting a Feeling," said Kale. "Something about her
looks familiar."

"Well, well, well," Captain Ann said. "Quite a motley crew
my baby sister has assembled."

"Her *sister?*" Jaundice said.

"Yer *sister?*" Lefty said to Delilah.

"Well, sink me!" said Peg. "This is quite a development."

"That's why she looks familiar," Kale said, snapping her fingers. "I see the resemblance now."

"Yer not me sister anymore," Delilah growled to Captain Ann. "I disowned ye when ye set me adrift."

"I set you adrift because you were stealing from me," Captain Ann reminded her. "And because you were an all-around pain in the biscuits. Everywhere I go now, I hear you're trying to track me down. Still trying to pilfer whatever's mine instead of finding your own treasure. And still wearing that silly fake eye patch."

"Shut yer trap!" Delilah said, stomping on the deck. "Shut it!"

"Make me," said Captain Ann, her hands on her hips.

Delilah brandished her cutlass. "Don't think I won't!"

Captain Ann chuckled. "Haven't changed much, have you?" she said. "Well, I have. I've gone legit now; I'm a privateer, which means I have a letter of marque from the queen, which means I have the authority to bring you in, for stealing, and kidnapping, and terrorizing the seven seas, and whatever other bratty mischief you've been up to. Besides, Mom and Dad are worried sick about you. You never visit, you never write . . ."

"Well, *laa-dii-daa*, Miss Privateer," said Delilah, sticking out her tongue.

"I have an offer for you, sister," Captain Ann said. "Surrender yourself to *The Booty Myth* and we'll leave your crew alone. Otherwise, it's not going to be pretty. You'll all be feeding the fish, mark my words."

"I'll never surrender!" Delilah shouted, tearing off her eye patch and flinging it at her sister.

"Suit yourself," said Captain Ann, turning to her crew. "Prepare to board!"

Instantly, the crew of *The Booty Myth* began jumping across and climbing onto *The Jolly Regina*. Swords and cutlasses and daggers and fists were drawn.

"Arrrgh!" growled the crew of *The Jolly Regina.*

"Grrrrr!" counter-growled the crew of *The Booty Myth.*

A terrific fight ensued, the likes of which the Bland Sisters, who were used to staring at wallpaper and watching the grass grow, had never seen. Delilah was sword fighting three privateers at a time. Lefty was swatting with her cat-o'-nine-tails. Scurvy was jumping on people's backs and biting their ears. Peg was swinging on a rope, using her wooden leg as a battering ram. Millie Mudd was hurling hardtack from the crow's nest. Fatima was grabbing her adversaries, often two at a time, and throwing them overboard.

For the first time ever, the Bland Sisters forgot to pretend they were sleeping. Amid all this action, they were too riveted to close their eyes.

"Maybe we should find a place to hide," whispered Kale, ducking as a dagger whizzed past.

"First, let's free our toes," said Jaundice. "Starting with mine."

Jaundice worked free their sailor's knots, then put her shoes and socks back on, then looked around.

"Ah, a dinghy!" she said.

"What did you call me?" asked Kale.

"Not you—the little boat over there," explained Jaundice. "We can hide inside!"

The Bland Sisters scrambled into the dinghy, which fit the two of them with only a bit of space to spare. They pulled a length of sailcloth over their heads, leaving just enough room to peek out and observe the exceptional display of swashbuckling.

Peg swung by on her rope, battering two privateers. But with her back turned, she didn't notice *The Booty Myth*'s first mate sneaking up on her with a dagger.

"Watch out, Peg!" Kale shouted. But the pirate-librarian was too far away to hear. Jaundice shoved her hands in her smock pockets while Kale covered her eyes. This was not going to end well.

ZZZZZWING!

"Ow! Owie, owie, ow, ow!" cried the first mate of *The Booty Myth*. She'd dropped her dagger and was clutching her hand, from which protruded a very shiny thumbtack.

Kale looked at Jaundice, who had a rubber band stretched across her thumb and forefinger like a slingshot.

"Yo-ho-ho!" said Jaundice. Kale patted her sister on the shoulder.

"Prepare to fire!" Captain Ann called back to the remaining crew on her ship.

"That's not fair!" Delilah shouted. "We don't have cannons!"

"Serves you right for spending all your doubloons on tracking down me and my treasure, and not arming your ship," Captain Ann said.

"What are cannons?" Kale whispered, reaching for Dr. Snoote.

"We're about to find out," said Jaundice.

Before long, *The Booty Myth* began firing on the *Regina*. A cannonball sailed through the air. It was coming right for Jaundice.

"Look out!" Kale said, but her sister didn't have time to duck. In an instant, Kale threw the dictionary with all her might, knocking the cannonball out of the way. In the process, Dr. Snoote tumbled overboard.

"Your dictionary!" Jaundice exclaimed. "What will you do without Dr. Snoote?"

"It was worth it," said Kale. "Besides, I can always get a new Dr. Snoote. There's only one of you."

Jaundice pulled back the sailcloth to get a closer look, and saw water seeping in from below deck where the cannonball had broken through.

"This isn't good," she said.

Fatima approached them, out of breath and sweating. One of her earlobes was bleeding. "I've been lookin' fer ye," she said.

"Are you all right?" Kale asked.

Fatima touched her ear. "Stupid monkey bit me by mistake," she said. "So I threw him overboard by mistake."

"The ship's going to sink," said Jaundice, showing Fatima the hole in the deck. The cannon fire echoing around them confirmed that the situation was growing worse.

"We've got to get ye two out of here," Fatima said, looking around. She took a deep breath and lifted the dinghy with the Bland Sisters inside.

"Where are we going?" Jaundice asked. But it soon became clear: Fatima was about to lower them over the side of the *Regina*, into the water.

Kale grabbed the cook's hand. "Aren't you coming with us?" she asked.

"Oh, ole Fatima has to lay off the hardtack a bit longer before she can fit in one of these little jolly boats," she said with a laugh. "Just keep rowin', and look out for land. Ye'll be fine, as long as ye stick together."

"And so will we. Don't you worry," said Peg, swinging down from her rope and putting her arm around Fatima. Then she handed Kale a large brass key.

"This is the key to me library, at Port Innastorm," Peg said. "You two can visit any time ye want. And ye can take out books now and then, if ye like. Just make sure ye return 'em on time; I might not be around to collect the overdue fee."

Kale slipped the key into her now-empty backpack. "We'll be honored," she said. For the first time, she and her sister found themselves holding back what they discovered were tears.

"Now, now," Fatima said gently. "The second rule of piratin' is there's no cryin' on deck. I only wish I had a little good-bye trinket fer ye both, to remember me by."

"It's okay," said Jaundice. "I have one for you."

She reached into her smock pocket and pulled out a hard ivory lump.

"What's this? A hardtack biscuit?" said Fatima, as Jaundice placed it in her hand. Then she turned it around and saw that it was a mermaid. A scrimshaw mermaid.

"It's the top of Smokey's pipe," the cook said, blinking in disbelief.

"I found it when we were cleaning last night," Jaundice explained. "It's yours, to remember how you stood up to those bullies."

"And how we made such a good chantey-writing team," added Kale.

"I'll treasure it," said Fatima, wiping her eyes. "Truly."

Jaundice and Kale gave Fatima and Peg each a hug good-bye. It was the first time they could remember giving a hug to anyone before, even each other; the experience would have been quite pleasant if the circumstances weren't so tragic. Then Fatima lowered them down.

"Good luck findin' yer parents!" called Fatima and Peg.

"Good luck staying alive!" shouted Jaundice and Kale.

Immediately, they began rowing. And though they heard cannon fire and shouts from the crews of both ships for a good long time, neither of the Bland Sisters looked back. They hoped to honor their friends by upholding the second rule of pirating: No cryin' on deck.

aliases |ˈālēəsəs| *plural noun*
assumed or false identities

Chapter Twenty-three

Many hours had passed, and the Bland Sisters were still rowing, wordlessly and determinedly. It was Kale who finally broke the silence.

"What's that?" she said. She pointed to a strip of brown and gray on the horizon.

"Don't get distracted," warned Jaundice. "We need to stay focused."

The Bland Sisters rowed quietly for another good ten minutes. The strip of brown and gray grew closer.

"Um, it looks like land," said Kale, squinting.

"Dr. Snoote had a definition for this, I think," Jaundice said, nearly out of breath.

"I do miss him," Kale said wistfully. "Even if he was old and musty, his definitions and sidebars were always so helpful. Like that bit with the compass—that was almost *too* clever, wasn't it?"

Though it was the right choice at the time, Kale was now experiencing serious regrets about abandoning her dictionary. She was at a loss without Dr. Snoote, her wordless yet wordful companion. It was as if, like Peg, she'd had a limb amputated.

Jaundice ignored her sister; this was no time for regrets.

"We think that's a strip of land, but it's called a *mirage*," she said. "It's a hallucination people often see when they're tired, or under stress. And we're both. Just ignore it and concentrate on rowing."

Kale looked at the horizon. Jaundice was almost always right.

"We're about to run aground," Kale announced.

And so they were. The Bland Sisters and their dinghy were now floating up to a length of sandy beach. With the last vestiges of their strength, Jaundice and Kale pulled the little boat up to the shore, fell face-first onto the sand, and promptly fell asleep.

Hours later, they woke up to the sound of seagulls crying and waves lapping against the dinghy. Kale grabbed a handful of sand and let it trickle through her fingers.

"I'm pretty sure this isn't a mirage," she said.

Jaundice stood up. Something had caught her eye. It was a large piece of wood, propped on its side and covered with sand. She brushed off the sign and gasped when the words on it became legible.

"We're on Gilly Guns Island!" Jaundice exclaimed.

"So we made it after all?" said Kale. "Talk about serendipity."

"We need to find our parents. They've been marooned here for a long time. Come on," said Jaundice.

"No thanks," said Kale. "I'll stay here." She had already begun counting grains of sand and didn't want to lose her place.

Jaundice took her sister by the arm. "I'm not leaving you here, silly. You can count sand later, when we get back."

Kale sighed. She was enjoying counting sand, as it gave her the same feeling she had when she watched the grass grow at home. She felt peaceful, almost sleepy, as if she were not really thinking, or using her brain at all.

The landscape was a bit rocky, so the Bland Sisters were slow-going in their exploration. They climbed to the top of what seemed to be the tallest outcropping and looked out. It was a sea of green: palm trees, vines, shrubs, and all sorts of exotic flowers, birds, and animals. A waterfall sparkled in the distance.

"Well," Jaundice said.

"Isn't that something?" added Kale.

They had never seen so much vegetation before. Other than the grass they watched grow each day, the Bland Sisters had one plant in their house, a ficus, which dropped its leaves whenever one of the sisters happened to walk by.

"All that green hurts my eyes," said Kale. "I much prefer brown."

"Or gray," said Jaundice, nodding.

"Shall we continue on the rocks?" asked Kale.

"Yes, let's," said Jaundice. The rocks were brown *and* gray, and therefore inviting.

Several yards ahead, the Bland Sisters caught sight of a break in the outcroppings. They saw a large hole there, large enough for each sister to walk through.

"I know what this is," Jaundice said. "It's a cave."

"Caves are supposed to be dark, and full of bats," recalled Kale.

"We have to go inside," Jaundice said. "Our parents could be in there."

Jaundice walked a few steps forward before realizing that her sister wasn't there. She turned around.

"Aren't you coming?" Jaundice asked.

"I'd rather count sand," said Kale.

"What's wrong?"

"I don't know that I even *want* to save them," Kale said, kicking a rock. "After all, they left us alone for all these years. Then they gave us to pirates, which was almost *fun*, until we almost *died*. I don't know much about parents, but I have a Feeling ours aren't exemplary."

Jaundice put her hands on her hips. "We came all this way. Now you don't want to find them?"

Kale shrugged and kept kicking the rock.

"They didn't just leave us alone. They left us a nice house," Jaundice reminded her sister. "They left us the mailbox, and arranged the sundries basket."

No response from Kale.

"Well, I'm going in," Jaundice said. "At least come along to keep me company."

Kale thought about this for a moment. "Fine," she said

finally, running to catch up with her sister. "But I'd still rather count sand."

The inside of the cave was not very deep, so the sun kept it from being very dark. Two boulders were set up almost like chairs, so the Bland Sisters sat down.

"I bet they sat right here," Jaundice said.

"I bet they really like clams," Kale said, kicking at the shells littering the floor.

"Maybe that's all they had to eat while they were sitting here," Jaundice said, "waiting for us to rescue them."

"Well, even if they were here, they're not anymore," Kale said.

"Maybe they're hiding out somewhere else now," Jaundice said. "Maybe they're in the green part of the island, where all the trees are."

Kale rolled her eyes, then went back to kicking shells. If they were at home, she'd be looking forward to her afternoon cheese sandwich. Instead, she was looking forward to a foreseeable future of wandering through jungles and eating nothing but clams. Of course, Kale had never been in a jungle or eaten a clam, but neither sounded appealing.

"Ow!" she exclaimed. Her foot kicked something larger than the other clamshells, and seemingly immovable.

It was a shell. But this shell had no earthly business being among a pile of clams. This was a large, creamy-yellow conch shell, polished to gleaming perfection, half-buried in the sandy cave floor. Kale got down on her hands and knees and started digging.

"What is it?" asked Jaundice.

"A souvenir," said Kale, dislodging the shell and brushing it off. "After everything we've been through, I'd at least like to bring home a nice memento. If we ever get home, that is."

It was really quite an impressive specimen. The illustration next to the definition of *shell* in Dr. Snoote's dictionary had been that of a clam, so the conch struck Jaundice as quite extraordinary. Particularly the tongue.

"The tongue is quite extraordinary," Jaundice remarked.

"What tongue?" Kale asked.

"There," Jaundice said, pointing at the opening in the shell. "That thing that looks like a bit of folded-up paper."

In fact, it *was* a bit of folded-up paper, as Kale discovered after poking at it tentatively. She pulled it out and unfolded it. Her eyes grew wide as she started reading.

"It's a letter," she said, looking at Jaundice. "For us."

Dear Darling Daughters, the letter began (with no small amount of alliteration),

You have found our hiding place here, and this letter! Bravo, you two!

In any case, apologies again, for leaving so abruptly all those years ago. As we've already told you in great detail, we thought we'd bid our past farewell when we'd assumed our aliases and settled into our modest life in Dullsville (and brought you both into the world). We were called back on what was supposed to be a brief errand—to rescue a colleague trapped in a shark cage—and on the return trip, we encountered some particularly nasty cannibals who wouldn't say no to having us stay for dinner. And then, after an expedition to the North Pole, followed by a jaunt across the Siberian tundra, we found ourselves a bit tied up, so to speak. Blah blah blah—we're sure we're boring you with this needless recap, as you've already heard these stories in the letters we've been sending each month. (Don't worry about not responding; we've moved around so much, we haven't really had a fixed mailing address.)

Of course, as we've been busy traveling the world, engaging in extraordinary pursuits as the zealous adventurers we are, we've missed you <u>desperately</u>, and we've been waiting for the day when you might be ready to join us—and that day has now come! Huzzah! ¡Hurra! Hourra! Alé! Heko!

By now you've realized that we deliberately led Deadeye Delilah to you, as we wanted her to show you an authentic, rollicking, piratical time, which would lead you here—and ultimately, to us! We hope your journey on The Jolly Regina (which we are sure you found as enlightening and entertaining as we did) has whetted your appetite for more suspense and excitement. We're sure you're eager to join us in our pursuit of fantastic sights and new experiences!

Looking forward to seeing you soon! A lifetime of adventure awaits!

All our love,

Mom and Dad

P.S. We've arranged for your transport off the island—just blow into this shell three times!

P.P.S. Before you leave the island, you should really explore the nature and wildlife preserve a bit—it's quite a treasure! Just watch out for the tigers and the quicksand and the snakes! Have fun! XOXOXOXO

The Bland Sisters sat on a rock in the cave and let all of this sink in.

"So . . . our parents are adventurers? With *aliases?*" Jaundice said.

"Does that mean our names are aliases, too?" asked Kale.

"I hope not. I can't imagine us being anything other than Bland," said Jaundice.

The sisters nodded. Nothing seemed truer.

"They say they sent us letters," Kale said. "What letters?"

"You didn't see any when you checked the mailbox?" Jaundice asked.

"I thought *you* were checking the mailbox," Kale said.

"I thought *you* were," said Jaundice.

The Bland Sisters blinked at each other. All this time, all these years, their parents had been corresponding with them, and they never knew it. Kale reread the letter, her fingers tracing each word as she went along.

"So all this was just their way of getting us out of the house?" she said.

"Now that's a plan," Jaundice said, nodding. "Very clever. Not to mention effective."

"We could have been keelhauled," Kale said. "Or spent the rest of our lives as indentured pirate servants."

"I suppose they'd consider that 'enlightening and entertaining,'" said Jaundice.

"So what do we do now?" asked Kale.

Jaundice picked up the conch shell. "There's only one thing to do," she said. "Unless you like the idea of being marooned here."

Kale took the shell from her sister and blew into it three times. Her lung capacity wasn't as impressive as Fatima's, but it was surprisingly significant. After the noise dissipated, the Bland Sisters looked at each other.

"Now, we wait," Kale said, clasping her hands and putting them in her lap.

"So I suppose you don't care to explore the preserve?" Jaundice asked.

"And behold all those flowers and plants and trees?" said Kale.

"And beware the tigers and quicksand and snakes," added Jaundice.

"Um, not interested," said Kale, going back to kicking shells.

"No," Jaundice said, joining her. "Me, neither."

materialistic |mə ̩ti(ə)rēə ̍listik| *adjective*
a tendency to focus on material
possessions, especially money

← ———— **Chapter Twenty-four** ————→

An hour later, the Bland Sisters heard a noise outside
the cave. It was the sound of a boat running aground.
Jaundice and Kale peeked out the cave opening.

"Yo-ho-ho!" bellowed a voice.

It was Captain Ann, standing on the bow of a large white
jolly boat. Inside the boat were several of her crew members,
as well as two familiar faces: Fatima and Peg. When they saw
the Bland Sisters step out of the cave, they leaped out of the
boat and ran over to them.

"Yer safe!" cried Fatima and Peg, giving each of the Bland
Sisters a constricting hug.

"You're alive!" cried Jaundice and Kale. Neither could define the emotion they were experiencing, which felt like a combination of happiness and relief.

"Fatima and I got sick of fightin', especially since we were sinkin' fast," Peg explained. "So she grabbed Delilah and handed her over to Captain Ann, in exchange for a cease-fire."

"Now she's in the brig of *The Booty Myth*," Fatima said. "Lefty, too."

"And as a reward for turning over my sister, I'm giving these two newly appointed privateers their own ship," Captain Ann said, clapping Fatima and Peg on the shoulder. "Most of the crew of the *Regina* will be joining them."

"They already elected Peg the captain," Fatima said, puffing out her sizable chest. "And me the first mate. Imagine that?"

"So, in a way, everything worked out," Jaundice said.

"Serendipity," Kale said. "That's what that is."

"Delilah violated the first rule of piratin'," Captain Peg said. "Steadfast loyalty to yer ship and yer shipmates, above everythin'. She'd rather risk all our lives than surrenderin' herself? Some captain she was."

"Plus, she was leadin' us all on a wild goose chase, lookin' for Cap'n Ann's booty," Fatima said.

"Wait," Kale said. "So there's no treasure?"

"There was," Captain Ann explained. "But I had to

give it up when I became a privateer, so I gave it to charity. Eventually, they used the money to create this nature and wildlife preserve." She waved her arm to indicate the sign the Bland Sisters had uncovered.

"So, in a way, the treasure really was on Gilly Guns Island," Jaundice said.

"And our parents were telling Delilah the truth about it," Kale added. "She was probably just expecting to find a chest filled with doubloons."

"My sister has always been a bit materialistic," Captain Ann said, picking a stray thread off her gold-embroidered jacket. "In any case, your parents enjoyed a good bit of exploring here before they called me for transportation off the island. Quite a pair, those two."

"Do you know where they went?" Kale asked.

"I should know," Captain Ann said. "I took them there. I have the directions they gave me back on the ship. Of course, they told me that whenever I found you, I should take you to them, or wherever in the world you'd like to go."

"So we can finally reunite with our parents," said Jaundice. "And join them on their adventures."

"Or have our own adventures, anywhere in the world," said Kale.

"Ooh, ye can go to the mountains!" Fatima said. "Or to the desert! Or to the rain forest!"

"Ye can go to Paris or Rome or London or Hong Kong," said Peg. "Or Hollywood!"

"Or you can stay awhile with me and sail the seven seas," said Captain Ann. "I could always use an assistant or two."

The Bland Sisters whispered to each other for a few moments. Then they looked at their pirate friends.

"We know exactly where we want to go," Kale said, rubbing her hands together.

"Right-o," said Jaundice. "But on the way, we'd like to make a little stop. To pick up some treasure."

"Sounds good to me," said Captain Ann. "Let's weigh anchor, mateys!"

anthropology |ˌanthrəˈpäləjē| *noun*
the study of humankind

Chapter Twenty-five

And so, Captain Ann and her crew and Captain Peg and First Mate Fatima rowed the Bland Sisters back to *The Booty Myth* and helped them seek out an amazing treasure trove—of books, at the library in Port Innastorm.

"I've never seen so many different-colored books before," Kale whispered, after using Captain Peg's key to unlock the door. It really was a grand display. Books were shelved floor to ceiling, just waiting to be read.

"Biology, sociology, anthropology, zoology," Jaundice said, reading off the signs marking each section. "Just about every 'ology' you could think of is here."

After a few more moments of exploring, the Bland Sisters came upon the same section simultaneously. It was marked REFERENCE.

"Ooh," said Kale.

"Ahh," said Jaundice.

The shelves in the reference section contained encyclopedias and dictionaries of just about every language and culture known to man, or woman. Though the selection seemed overwhelming at first, it was not long before the Bland Sisters discovered one very familiar volume.

"*Dr. Nathaniel Snoote's Illustrated Children's Dictionary!*" Kale exclaimed, embracing the book and twirling around. "Hello, old friend!"

PORT INNASTORM

Captain Ann appeared in the doorway.

"Knock-knock," she said. "I don't mean to rush you two, but we should probably be going in the next hour or so, if we want to make it before sunset."

"Captain Peg said we could take out books, if we like," Jaundice said to her sister. "Why don't we take Dr. Snoote? I know how you've missed him."

Kale looked at the old, familiar, musty dictionary. Then she looked at the shelves and shelves of books around her, which seemed to glitter, like the stars she and her sister saw from the deck of *The Jolly Regina*. She remembered Captain Peg's words.

Dictionaries are just words and meanings. Dry as sand. Books are filled with adventures and emotions and ideas!

Slowly, Kale let go of Dr. Snoote and put him back on the shelf.

"The fiction section is quite impressive," she noted, turning to her sister. "Maybe we should try a story, for a change."

"I'd be up for an adventure," suggested Jaundice.

"Where to next?" asked First Mate Fatima, doing a little jig. "Somewhere exotic?"

The Bland Sisters smiled at each other. They had the same, perfect destination in mind.

incinerator |inˈsinəˌrātər| *noun*
an apparatus for burning
garbage or waste

Epilogue

I t's nice to be home, isn't it?" said Jaundice, darning another sock.

"It is," said Kale, between bites of cheese sandwich. "Terribly."

"I couldn't think of another place I'd rather be," said Jaundice.

That's exactly what the Bland Sisters told Captain Ann and Captain Peg and First Mate Fatima. Despite the exciting array of options laid before them, as well as their parents' invitation to join them on their travels, Jaundice and Kale had decided that they belonged back in their little house on the road to Dullsville. In fact, they conveyed these very sentiments in a letter they left with their pirate friends, to be delivered to their parents at their earliest opportunity.

After much discussion and revision, it ended up going like this:

Dear Mom and Dad,

Thanks very much for introducing us to the pirates. Though we faced peril on more than a few occasions (including a very painful near keelhauling); suffered food poisoning from a questionable stew; were forced into menial, deck-scrubbing labor; were threatened with a cat-o'-nine-tails; endured nasty burlap chafings; and lost our beloved friend and dictionary, Dr. Snoote, we know we would not have met First Mate Fatima or Captain Peg or Captain Ann were it not for this experience, and so, we are admittedly grateful. As Captain Peg might say, ye never turn down a moment of serendipity.

Of course, we hope we are reunited soon. But to be honest, we're really not interested in going on another adventure. We're physically and mentally exhausted, and frankly, we'd rather stay home; it's so much cozier here than any kind of adventure, with far less chance of messiness, injury, or death.

When you decide to take a break from your travels, we hope you'll join us. We can all spend some quality time together, eating cheese sandwiches and watching the grass grow . . . doesn't that sound nice?

Hope we'll be seeing you soon, and that you're well (and, more important, alive).

Your daughters,

Jaundice & Kale

P.S. We had a little problem with checking the mail recently, but it's all cleared up now.

P.P.S. Captain Ann, Captain Peg, and First Mate Fatima said they'd keep in touch—we look forward to hearing more about their travels, and yours, as we won't be doing any of our own any time soon.

Unfortunately, the Bland Sisters did not have very good luck in retrieving the correspondence their parents had initially sent them. Over the years, Mr. Bartleby, their mail carrier, had noted the overflowing mailbox and had transferred all the unanswered correspondence to the DDLO (Dullsville Dead Letter Office), where it had eventually met with the incinerator. Shortly thereafter, Mr. Bartleby resigned, citing exhaustion and postal-traumatic stress.

"It really is too bad, about that mail," Jaundice said. "It would have been nice to learn more about our parents."

"And it would have been nice to read about their adventures," said Kale. "Without having to actually *participate* in them."

"At least we've had a new book," said Jaundice.

"Yes," said Kale. "That's something."

The Bland Sisters had very much enjoyed the book they checked out from the Port Innastorm Library, per Captain Peg's invitation. It was a story about two brothers called the Nubbins Twins who find themselves on a submarine 19,999 leagues under the sea. Kale found it brilliantly plotted, and Jaundice was struck by the ingenious illustrations.

"We need to return it to the library soon," Kale reminded her sister. "It's almost overdue."

"What should we take out next?" asked Jaundice. "Another adventure? Or a mystery, perhaps? I might like a good mystery."

"I remember seeing an interesting dictionary there, in the reference section," said Kale. "*Ye Olde Pirate's Dictionary*, I think it was called."

"I thought we were through with dictionaries for now," said Jaundice. "Not to mention pirates."

"We should be fully informed. They could stop by again," Kale noted.

"I doubt it," said Jaundice. "It's not like our parents are

going to lure us out by sending *another* pirate here. Or anyone else, for that matter. We've made it clear we're not interested in adventure. Not in *real* life, anyway."

Kale nodded. Jaundice was almost always right.

Shortly after this exchange, Jaundice went into the kitchen to fix a cheese sandwich. The cheese had arrived in the sundries basket that very morning, and it was of the white variety, the Bland Sisters' new favorite. Jaundice had taken to putting the cheese between two hardtack biscuits, which she'd made with her own extra-stale recipe.

As her sister ate, Kale took another sock from the darning basket, and began humming a tune as she worked. The tune sounded not unlike a chantey.

Post Script

Just as the Bland Sisters settled back into their seemingly
content and unassuming existence, the village of
Dullsville went on per usual. In particular, the Dullsville
Post Office engaged in its daily functioning, receiving and
processing mail from hither and yon. The letters and packages
were stamped and sorted by Miss Penny Post, Mr. Bartleby's
former assistant and new replacement. Miss Post placed the
sorted mail in her satchel, mounted her bicycle, and went
about her deliveries.

Miss Post felt uneasy as she pedaled, and not just because
her back bicycle wheel was in need of tightening. On this

particular day, she had a letter in her satchel for none other than the Bland Sisters. It was in a stained envelope stamped with foreign postage, and it smelled faintly of spices. The handwriting on the envelope was all too familiar to Miss Post; she had seen it many times before, on a variety of other letters and packages, before the incinerator turned them all to ash. Mr. Bartleby had resigned soon after the incineration and left Dullsville; the last thing he said, when asked to provide a forwarding address, was "I prefer not to."

Miss Post reached the Bland Sisters' mailbox, placed the letter inside, and lifted the red metal flag to show that a delivery had been made. Before she got back on her squeaky bicycle and continued with her daily deliveries, she said a little prayer that this mail might be opened.

For, after all, a letter can change one's life; it can deliver grand adventure, or grave misfortune, or a great discovery. Or, sometimes, even all three.

ACKNOWLEDGMENTS

Many thanks to my family, friends, and colleagues, particularly Barry Goldblatt, a cutthroat pirate/agent with a heart of gold; the swashbuckling crew at Abrams/ Amulet, including Tamar Brazis, editor and pirate queen; Jen Hill, a genuine treasure; Anika Denise, Jamie Michalak, and Kristen Tracy, the saucy beauties who keep my writing shipshape; Jenna LaReau, anything-but-bland sister; and Scott and Camden Bowers, aka me hearties.

Kara LaReau was born and raised in Connecticut. She received her master's in fine arts in writing, literature, and publishing from Emerson College in Boston, Massachusetts, and later worked as an editor at Candlewick Press and at Scholastic Press. She is the author of *Ugly Fish* and *Otto: The Boy Who Loved Cars*, illustrated by Scott Magoon; *No Slurping, No Burping!: A Tale of Table Manners*, illustrated by Lorelay Bové; and *The Infamous Ratsos*, illustrated by Matt Myers. Kara lives in Providence, Rhode Island, with her husband and son.

Jen Hill is the illustrator of *Diana's White House Garden* by Elisa Carbone; *Doing Her Bit: A Story About the Woman's Land Army of America* by Erin Hagar; *Spring for Sophie* by Yael Werber; and *Be Kind* by Pat Zietlow Miller. She is also the author and illustrator of *Percy and TumTum: A Tale of Two Dogs.* Jen is a graduate from the Rhode Island School of Design, where she studied children's book illustration with David Macaulay and Judy Sue Goodwin Sturges. She lives in Brooklyn, New York, with her husband and her intern, Little Bee, who is very helpful for a cat.

Read on for a look
at Jaundice and Kale's
next adventure in
The Uncanny Express!

THE UNINTENTIONAL CAST OF CHARACTERS

Jaundice & Kale

Frank Harold

Magique

Hugo Fromage

Countess Goudenoff

Vera Dreary

Cecily Springwell

Desmond Goode

Colonel McRobb

Kirk Hatchett

TO CLEAN YOUR TOILET PROPERLY,
add ¼ cup chlorine bleach to the bowl
and let it stand before scrubbing.
Don't forget to flush!

Chapter One

It was a particularly uneventful afternoon in at least one house on the road to Dullsville. To say that it was particularly uneventful is saying a lot, as this house was occupied by none other than the Bland Sisters, Jaundice and Kale.

You might tell the Bland Sisters apart in several ways.

First, Jaundice prefers to dress in gray, while Kale favors brown.

Second, Kale wears her hair parted on the side, while Jaundice parts hers in the middle.

Third, Jaundice is left-handed while Kale is right-handed.

Fourth, Kale is seldom seen without her backpack, in which she currently carries *Tillie's Tips*, a worn little paperback featuring page after page of housekeeping advice, supplemented with helpful (if slightly dated) black-and-white illustrations. Kale came across this particular title at the Port Innastorm Library several weeks ago and has already renewed it twice. She finds *Tillie's Tips* incredibly helpful—and, of course, she finds comfort in knowing that there is someone out there who is more obsessed with cleaning than she is.

Fifth, Jaundice is known to wear a smock featuring an inordinate number of pockets. She tends to pop items in her pockets at random, providing herself with such treasures as a lone shoelace, two or three paper clips, a handful of clothespins, and a slightly damp kitchen sponge. Jaundice does not always remember to empty her pockets before her smock goes into the wash, much to the continued chagrin of Kale, who does the laundry.

Other than these few distinctions, the Bland Sisters are just about the same.

Jaundice and Kale pride themselves on their exacting routine. After breakfast (plain oatmeal with skim milk, a cup of weak, tepid tea on the side) they tend to their business of darning other people's socks, which takes the better part of the day. Each allows herself one ten-minute break, during which she eats a cheese sandwich on day-old bread (or hardtack biscuits, thanks to a recipe the Bland Sisters recently acquired) and drinks a glass of flat soda while gazing out the window, watching the grass grow.

The Bland Sisters look forward most to the evenings, when they entertain themselves by thinking of numbers divisible by three then staring at the wallpaper until they fall asleep. Not long ago, they enjoyed the nighttime ritual of reading a dictionary aloud to each other; since that dictionary left their possession, they have decided to broaden their horizons.

It should be mentioned that Jaundice and Kale have parents. Evidently, they are adventurers of some sort and send the Bland Sisters accounts of their travels whenever they can get to a mailbox. This is fine with Jaundice and Kale, as they much prefer reading about adventures to actually having them. And besides, they are sure their parents will return any day now. Certainly, one can only be away from the comforts and routines of home for so long.

In any event, not only was nothing happening to the Bland Sisters on this particular day, it seemed as if *less* than nothing was happening. Their business of darning other people's socks had been slow that week, so Jaundice and Kale had already finished mending the few they'd been given. The daily oatmeal and weak, tepid tea and cheese sandwiches and flat soda had been consumed, the grass-growing had been observed, and the Bland Sisters were several hours away from bedtime and its accompanying rituals. Nevertheless, they succeeded in passing the time; Jaundice found solace in tying knots in a piece of string (knots had become her new hobby, ever since the Bland Sisters had been tied up by their toes and nearly keelhauled by pirates), and Kale occupied herself with her favorite of all chores: cleaning the bathroom, which she accomplished with her implement of choice, an old toothbrush.

It was in the middle of scrubbing the inside of the toilet tank that Kale suddenly dropped the aforementioned toothbrush. Normally, this sort of mishap would cause her to cry out, as no one, not even a Bland Sister, wants to have to reach into the murky waters of a toilet tank to retrieve anything. But in this case, Kale was too preoccupied to make any sort of noise.

"Jaundice?" she finally called out to her sister.

"Yes, Kale?" Jaundice replied, working on a particularly difficult knot.

"I'm having a Feeling," Kale announced.

Jaundice sighed, looking up at the ceiling.

Her sister was always having Feelings. It was very

trying. Not so long ago, Kale had a Feeling, and the Bland Sisters were subsequently kidnapped by the aforementioned pirates, forced into menial labor, and stranded (if only temporarily) on a deserted island. Sometimes, Jaundice wished her sister would keep her Feelings to herself.

"Did you hear me?" Kale asked, emerging from the bathroom.

"I heard you," said Jaundice. "So what kind of Feeling are we talking about this time?"

"I'm having a Feeling something's about to happen," said Kale.

"And what happened after you started having this Feeling?" Jaundice asked.

Kale thought for a moment. "I dropped my toothbrush into the toilet tank," she said.

"A toothbrush in the toilet tank," said Jaundice. "That *is* quite a happening."

"I don't think that's it," said Kale, closing her eyes.

"And why not?" asked Jaundice.

"Because I'm still having the Feeling," said Kale.

"Is the toothbrush still in the toilet tank?" asked Jaundice.

Kale nodded.

"Well, there you go," said her sister. "You'd better go fish it out."

"What a relief," said Kale, rolling up one sleeve. "I was really starting to think something more serious was going to happen. You know, like last time. With the pirates."

"Perish the thought," said Jaundice, getting up from the couch. "I'm going to go out to the mailbox."

"But today's my turn to get the mail," said Kale.

"Given where your hands have been all afternoon," her sister said, "I think you should sit this one out."

"Good idea," said Kale. Jaundice was almost always right.